The Secret of
Council Hill

*For Elizabeth &
John
Keep Reading
Hap Arnold*

The Secret of
Council Hill

Written By
Hap Arnold

Illustrated By
Kieran Wathen

For Sarah and Nathan

Contents

THE GUEST ROOM

Yellow sunlight slipped between the blinds, painting stripes on Beth's face. Squinting, she pulled the covers over her head. It was useless; she was awake. Beth rose, stretching, and the floor creaked as she shuffled to the window. Another perfect day greeted her. A light breeze blew the branches of a slender holly, waving just outside the billowing curtains. The air smelled new and green. Beth should have been delighted, but she just felt grumpy. The sun had yanked her back to this little room while she was deep in a lovely dream.

In her dream, she was nibbling delicate chocolates on the high deck of a great ocean liner. White seabirds whirled as her hair whipped back in the salty breeze. She didn't know where the giant ship was going, but was sure it was somewhere exciting. She was watching her parents emerge from their stateroom. They were strolling toward her, hand in hand and smiling when she woke up.

"Now I'll never know where we were heading," she said to herself, glancing around the bedroom. This wasn't where she belonged, stuck away in Aunt Lily's guest quarters. Beth sighed, as she appraised her summer home, wondering when her parents would be back from their long trip abroad. The guest room was about as far away from a swanky ocean cruiser as you could get. It was tidy and comfortable, but very plain. As Beth thought of the long waiting days ahead,

1

another icicle of envy stabbed her stomach. It wasn't fair. For her the ship was just a dream, but her parents were actually on board, sailing to places that she would probably never get to see. It wasn't right. Beth made a promise to herself that if someday she had a child, she would never say they were too young to travel, and send them off like a pet to a kennel.

Beth chewed on her lip as she pulled on her tee shirt and snapped her overalls. She caught a glimpse of her face, hung and sorrowful, in the small mirror above the desk. She bared her teeth and growled at her reflection, flaring her nostrils. Her mouth grimaced like a cornered wolverine. It made her giggle, and she sat and made faces for a couple of minutes, using her fingers to pull her nose up like a pig, propping her ears forward with her thumbs. Her face started to ache from stretching, and her fingers left pink marks on her cheeks. She brushed her hair back, and slipped out of the room to find her shoes.

The house was quiet and still. As she walked down the hall, she heard noises from her cousin Ryan's room. Ryan was a little older, and thought he knew everything. Beth decided to investigate. His door was a little ajar, and she took a peek inside. Ryan's black hair was ruffled from sleep, standing straight up like a ceremonial headdress. He had an old robe thrown over his shoulders like a cape and his jeans were tucked into his father's old combat boots, about eighty sizes too big. He was swinging around the fake sword he made from old lumber trim, brandishing a shield that was normally a rubber trash can lid.

"Ha Ha!" he said, clomping onto the bed, pounding the sword hilt on his skinny chest, then beating it on his shield. He twisted his face into a warrior's scowl so comical that Beth fell into the room, laughing. Ryan stood there confused and surprised, the bed squeaking under his weight. The look on his face was even funnier, and Beth gasped for air.

"Get out of my room, you little spy!" Ryan shouted, turning pink. He dropped the sword and shield as he hopped down from the bed. "Haven't you ever heard of knocking?"

"You forgot to take off your helmet," Beth chuckled, pointing at his hair.

"Get out of my room! You've got your own room. Leave me alone!"

"What's all this shouting about?" Aunt Lily stood in the doorway. "Lower your voice, Ryan. Can't you speak nicely to Beth?" She wrinkled her forehead at Ryan.

"She's spying on me, Mom!"

"I'm sure she's just looking for something to do, aren't you?" Aunt Lily gave Beth's shoulders a squeeze. Her Aunt's long fingers smoothed her hair.

"Well, she can look somewhere else besides my room." Ryan mumbled. Aunt Lily pursed her lips at him, and turned back to Beth.

"Did you sleep well, sugar?" She flashed another smile at her young niece. Beth nodded her head. Beth always felt shy around Aunt Lily, even though she liked her enormously. "Why don't you come on downstairs, and have some breakfast with me. I'm on laundry patrol. You two gather up your things and bring them down."

Aunt Lily scooped up a discarded shirt, some torn jeans, and a few crumpled socks. She left the two children, Ryan glowering darkly at his cousin. Beth had the urge to stick her tongue out at him. Instead, she raised her chin and spun on her heel, flouncing out of the room.

Ryan stepped out of the heavy boots and threw the robe into a heap in the corner. He was not happy. Since Beth had come to visit, nothing was the same. They argued about everything. When he tried to explain things to Beth, she was too stubborn to listen. Even when Beth knew Ryan was right, she'd just cross her arms and pout her lip or stick her fingers in her ears. Ryan was totally exasperated with his cousin.

Ryan gathered up the rest of his dirty clothes out of the hamper. He looked out the window at Brad's house across the street. The windows were blank and the "For Sale" sign in the

4

front lawn had fallen over. Brad was Ryan's best friend since the first grade. The moving vans had left two weeks ago, right after the last day of school. Brad said the move meant a big promotion for his mom, and they had to go. It was just one more thing to ruin his summer. He pulled on some shorts and a shirt from the heap of clothes, lugging the heavy pile downstairs.

Beth sat on a wooden stool, kicking her feet and holding one of Aunt Lily's pancakes in her hand, a perfect half-circle bitten out of the top. Ryan's mom chuckled over her coffee mug as he staggered down the stairs under the pile of laundry, flopping it on the kitchen floor next to the washer.

"I guess it has been a while. Are those clean, Ryan?" She pointed at his shirt and shorts.

"They're clean enough."

"They've got ketchup on them from yesterday, son. Go on up and change."

"This is what I want to wear, O.K.? I don't have anything clean anyway."

Beth just watched them with wide eyes, smirking at Ryan when Aunt Lily turned back to the stove. He ignored Beth, and pulled up a stool at the corner of the kitchen counter. Ryan's mom set some fresh pancakes and a tub of butter in front of him. Beth slid the syrup over.

"What are you two going to do today?" Aunt Lily asked, blowing on her coffee. Ryan rolled his eyes and mumbled, shrugging his shoulders. "I hope that means you're going to do something outside, because it's a beautiful day, and I've got things to do in this house. Why don't you two go for a ride, out to the park or something. I know, what about that new playground in town?"

"I don't care. Whatever." Ryan murmured, syrup on his lip.

"We can go down to the park?" Beth asked, her parents rarely let her leave the house without extreme supervision.

"Sure, Beth. Just stay close to Ryan, he knows the rules. He'll look after you, won't you Ryan?" She handed him a napkin.

"I guess." Ryan wiped his mouth, Aunt Lily put a finger under his chin and gently raised his face to meet her eyes.

"Excuse me, son?"

"Yes, mom. I'll look after Beth."

BETH AND RYAN

"It wasn't my fault, Ryan. It was an accident." Beth hurried to catch up with Ryan. Heat shimmered off the parking lot asphalt, and Ryan's face was flushed as he pushed his mangled bike. A new scrape on his knee and shin seeped through oily dirt. Beth felt gritty sweat on her neck and forehead.

"Why'd you even have to come along. You're such a pain." Ryan winced as he stepped over the curb, wheeling his bike onto the sidewalk. They had been riding around all day, trying to find something they both wanted to do. They couldn't even agree what to do for lunch, so they just skipped it. The heat and frustration made them both mean as snakes.

They were in the parking lot in front of Cooper's, the department store Beth's family owned. Mr. Thompson, the manager, was outside with a delivery. He saw her and waved, but Beth didn't wave back. She was silent for a moment as Ryan checked his bike for damage. Straddling the front wheel, he wrenched the handlebars back into alignment. He rolled forward a few feet, testing it, and they continued walking their bikes in angry silence. Ryan's bike made a scraping sound as the chain rubbed against the guide.

"I said I was sorry," Beth piped. "You jumped in front. I couldn't turn in time."

"You're too slow. I swear, I could walk faster than you ride." Ryan bent over the bike, yanking the chain guard back into shape. "Look what you did to my bike."

"Maybe if you weren't showing off, it wouldn't have happened."

"Maybe if you stayed home, it wouldn't have happened." Ryan glared at Beth.

"It's not my home, and I don't want to be there," she shouted.

"Well, I don't want you there either. Nobody asked me if you could come and waste my summer, so your folks wouldn't have to drag you around on their vacation."

"Well it wasn't my idea! If you think I wanted to stay here, you're crazy!" Beth shouted. Shoppers turned, staring at the kids.

"Calm down." Ryan climbed on his bike. "Don't have a tantrum. I swear, you are such a baby." He shook his head, knowing how much Beth hated it when he called her that. She was so angry, she couldn't talk. She just spluttered and turned even redder. "I'm going back home," Ryan added. "You don't want to do anything I want to do. You're just too young."

"Ha!" Beth managed to blast out. "Two years! You're only two years older and you talk like you're going to college or something. You go on home, Ryan, where you can be all alone. Where are all your friends, huh? The truth is, you don't have any. You're too much of a jerk." Now Ryan was angry. Beth hopped on her bike and rode away. Ryan pedaled quickly to catch up.

"Who wants to hang around when I've got to baby-sit you? You never want to do anything fun. If I want to do something, you either don't know how, or you're too scared."

"I am not." Beth flashed her eyes at Ryan. "I'll do anything you'll do."

"Wrong! I know something you won't do."

"What?"

"Go into Council Wood," Ryan sneered.

"I thought nobody was allowed in there."

"I've been… Lots of times."

"Sure you have."

"It's true! Brad and I went in there to find a place for a hide out."

"Oh yeah, and Brad just happens to not be here, right?"

"I'll prove it. I'll go in again and show you. It's just an old forest." They both slowed their bikes and stopped. Beth's cheeks were still a little red, but her voice grew quieter.

"Debbie told me her older brother went in there and saw some kind of creature slinking around. She said that people have gone in and never come out."

"It's haunted… If you believe in that sort of thing. Ask anybody. People see and hear bizarre stuff around there all the time, especially near the hill. It doesn't bother me. I think they're all just stories to frighten people away. It's government property or something. I knew you'd be too scared to go."

She pushed off and pedaled down the sidewalk. They rode in silence for a moment before Beth answered. "Are you daring me?"

"No, you're afraid of everything. You won't do it."

"If you go, I will. I don't care." Beth set her jaw. She pedaled hard, pushing in front of Ryan.

"We'll see. Let's leave the bikes at the house. Let me clean this scrape up, and we'll go," he called after her.

"Now?" She turned and looked back at him, coasting.

"Yeah, right now. Unless you can't handle that," Ryan sneered, catching up to Beth.

"Fine."

Into Council Wood

An old wrought-iron fence bordered Founder's Park. Black metal bars shaped like elaborate ivy twisted into sharp points above the street. Stone posts carved from massive blocks stood guard, solid and tall on either side of the park entrance. Blackbirds perched on the iron ivy. They bobbed and squawked as Beth raced up to the park, Ryan trailing. He clacked a stick against the fence as he jogged along. Just inside the gate, the statue of Colonel Weston peered at the entrance. Beth hopped on the side of the fountain basin, beneath the bronze gaze of the gallant Colonel. She placed each foot carefully, arms out like a tightrope walker. Ryan strolled up behind her, the stick over his shoulder, and Beth jumped down before he could push her in. They trotted down a pebbly path, crossing the wide lawn to Beech Creek.

The grass was thick and the air cool near the brook. Ryan thrashed the reeds with his stick, and startled frogs plopped into the stream. Beth lobbed stones into the water, walking higher along the bank.

"Quit it! You're splashing me!" Ryan pointed his stick at Beth. She made a face, but stopped throwing rocks. Ryan trudged up the path as the stream bed carved deeper into the bank. The trees gradually became older and taller, looming high above them, blocking the afternoon sun.

"Are we out of the park now?" Beth picked at the moss on a great oak.

"Almost. Up here at the fence, we jump over and into the woods." Ryan hopped up and swung on a lower branch, shaking the tree. "There's a path we can follow. You don't have to be scared."

"I'm not scared. I was just curious." She trotted down the path quickly to prove it.

As the trail bent away, they crept up a grassy hill. Climbing over a wooden rail fence marking the border of the park, they crossed a dirt road and came to a rusty barbed wire fence. Ignoring the shotgun speckled "No Trespassing" signs, they gingerly stepped over the fence where a great limb had fallen, crushing the wires to the ground.

Now the great old trees crowded on each other and the forest floor was thick with fallen branches and leaves. Tiny patches of blue sky were the only sign of daylight. The forest was completely silent and still. Bumps stood out on Beth's forearms as she looked into the dark thicket of gray trunks ahead.

"Council Wood," Ryan announced. "Do you want to go further, or have you had enough?"

"I don't care," Beth said, trying to sound bored. "Whatever you want. It's just an old forest."

"You don't believe the stories?" Ryan raised an eyebrow and picked up a pine cone. Just then a breeze stirred the trees and a rushing, clattering sound swept around the kids. Beth looked around nervously and Ryan chuckled at her unease. She set her jaw and squinted at him. "There's no such thing as ghosts, or any of that stuff, but..."

"But what?" Ryan leaned against a tree, peeling the bark from a branch.

"We're not supposed to be here. You're going to get us into trouble."

"It's O.K. if you're worried. Most little kids wouldn't even have come this far." He looked up to grin at Beth, but she had turned and was marching along a faint trail in the undergrowth, deeper into the woods. Ryan hurried after her.

They hiked in silence, Beth tromping in front. Ryan followed her, his hands in his pockets. For a while, they saw cans and bottles littering the way, but soon these signs of civilization disappeared, and the path became fainter.

They wound deeper into the whispering trees, and minutes stretched into hours. Ryan looked around, realizing this was the farthest he had been into the wood. Searching for a familiar landmark, he bumped into Beth. The path was gone. They stood in front of a massive, gnarled maple. Squirrels chased each other around the trunk, chattering.

The trees were farther apart here, making a sort of clearing, and they saw gray clouds cresting the high crown of Council Hill, much closer now. A grumble of thunder rolled across the wood.

13

"Let's head back," Ryan said. They had walked longer than he wanted to. Now he wondered if they would make it back before dinner.

"Sure, if you're scared," Beth mocked Ryan. "What's wrong? Worried about a little thunder?"

"C'mon, Beth, it's getting late." He turned and started back down the path. Beth sighed, rolling her eyes as she followed him. Secretly, she was relieved they were heading back. The farther she walked into the forest, the more she felt as if someone was watching her. Several times, she had the urge to spin and look behind her. The thought of Ryan grinning and chuckling was the only thing that kept her going. The silent, heavy air made her feel tired and slow.

They had walked for some time when Ryan stopped. "I don't remember two paths here." He knelt on the ground, rubbing his cheek.

"I didn't notice that either," Beth said quietly, thunder trailing behind her.

Ryan rocked on his heels, remembering hiking with his Dad a long time ago. His father had crouched like this, tapping on the ground, reminding Ryan that paths can be tricky. While you're looking ahead, other paths may be connecting behind you, so when you make your way back, you find a split that wasn't there before. The children puzzled over which trail led back to the park. Ryan had given up on the idea of trying to get home by dinner, and was just hoping that they would still have daylight.

"I think we came from the one on the right. This tree looks familiar." Beth laid her hand on a peeling birch.

"All these trees look the same. Are you sure?" Ryan rubbed his fingers in the loose leaves on the ground. "This path looks more worn to me. Let's take the left one."

"I'm pretty sure, Ryan. I'm going this way."

"I'm telling you, more people have been down the other trail. We need to stay together."

"Why? We're always together. I thought you were sick of me. Now you can be all by yourself. I'll find my own way." Beth stomped off down the path. Ryan just stood and watched her. A few steps later, Beth was sorry she had left him. She turned to see if he was following, and caught a glimpse of Ryan shrugging his shoulders as he set off down the opposite trail. The wind began to pick up and the trees shook. Being alone was the last thing Beth wanted, but she could not go back to Ryan's smug face. She glanced through the heavy branches at the darkening sky. Sighing, she trotted off down the path.

She wandered for some time following a small brook, and the path ended at a rocky pool. She could smell rain and the clouds above rolled by quickly. The wind made the leaves flip their pale sides up and Beth felt frightened. She rushed off back to the first path. Now it was getting dark and it was harder to see the trail. Several times she lost it completely and had to backtrack, bent at the waist, scanning the ground. By the time she had made it back to the familiar birch tree, she was sweating and scared. Everything was turning pink and gray as the sun began to set. She called for Ryan, but there was no answer. Her voice sounded thin and muffled, tiny and lost.

When Beth looked up, she could see light in the sky, but it had grown gray and shadowy on the forest floor. She had to go slower, still slipping on hidden stones. She was not sure if she was still on the path, and her breath came quicker with fear. She decided to let herself cry a little. She tried to do so quietly because she did not like the way her voice sounded in these woods. The trunks of the trees had turned into shadows, and the shadows had turned into darkness. Pausing to sniffle, she heard leaves rustling and crackling behind her. Spinning around, she saw a dark shape looming behind her.

"Beth?" Ryan's voice greeted her just as she was about to scream.

"Ryan!" Her voice was happy and relieved.

"Are you O.K., Beth?"

"No! I'm lost! Where are we?" Relieved and spent, she leaned against him. He patted her awkwardly and was silent for a moment.

"I was hoping you would know," he said softly. Sniffling, Beth pushed away from him.

"This was stupid! Why did we come?" Beth shouted. "You said you knew these woods! Now we're stuck! What are we going to do?"

"You went too far! Nobody goes this deep into these woods. It's not my fault, I was just following you. You had to be the smart…"

"Quiet! What's that there?" Beth pointed down the path.

"What?" Ryan turned and squinted, following Beth's finger.

"There! There!" A dark shadow slipped from trunk to trunk just off to their right. It grew, sliding silently nearer.

Laughing Cloud

Too afraid to scream, Beth grabbed Ryan, digging her fingers into his arm.

"Ow!" he shouted, forgetting his fear for a moment. The shadow stopped. It was tall and thin. Even in the poor light, they could see it was a man.

"Why are you here, in my forest?" A low but soft voice issued from the dark figure.

"We... uh... we didn't know it was your forest," Ryan stammered.

"Sir," Beth added.

"Hmmm. I suppose it isn't mine, but I belong to this place, and you do not. Others who do not belong have been here, but not so young, and not this far. And they do not stay when the sun falls."

"We'll be happy to leave anytime, if you'll just show us which way to go."

"Where do you wish to be?"

"Home," Beth said, and her throat felt tight. "Please, show us how to get home."

"Ah. Well, I know the way to my home, but not yours."

"Do you know the way to the park?" Ryan asked. "Can you take us there?" He had to shout over the wind. Lightning

18

lit the forest canopy like a strobe, and they caught a gaunt silver outline of the figure before them. He was tall and lanky, with long hair. His face remained in shadow.

The man chuckled. "You two have wandered a long way from the statue. This storm is eager to play, and will have some fun with you before you get back to the park. We are closer to my home, you can take shelter there. Here, hold on to my bow. The sun is asleep now. You must choose a branch for your friend to hold on to." Ryan picked up a branch and held it out to Beth. The figure moved closer. There was just enough light to see he wore faded and patched overalls. He had a great mane of long black hair shot with gray, hanging over deep eyes. His hands were large and rough. He held one out to Ryan.

"I am Laughing Cloud. What are you called?"

"I'm Ryan Johnson," he said formally, and his hand disappeared into Laughing Cloud's. "This is my cousin, Beth Cooper." She nodded and shook his hand as well.

"I knew a farmer named Johnson, east of the hill." The tall man said.

"We live in the town, in Anderson Acres," Ryan said, puzzled.

"It is a common name. I also once made trade with Cooper in the village." Laughing Cloud said, looking at Beth. His voice was soft and rumbling. "They trade fair."

"That's probably my dad, but he hasn't worked on the floor for a long time."

"It has been a long time, Beth Cooper. Let's hurry on. I'll try to take small steps." Laughing Cloud held out a strong, slender bow of light wood, Ryan held it securely, and his finger accidentally struck the string. A note sprang up as if a violin had been plucked. The tall man smiled and led the children up a slope to their right. Despite what he said,

19

Laughing Cloud moved quickly. Linked together, the children hurried to keep up with his great strides.

It was pitch black beneath the trees. Beth held on to the crooked branch connecting her to Ryan, stumbling on the uneven ground. Laughing Cloud's tall form pressed on before them. They walked in silence for a long time. The storm clouds broke open for a few minutes, and the moon rose. A few silver rays slipped to the forest floor as darker clouds built over the hill again. A calm gripped the forest, and Ryan could feel the storm growing, building up pressure like a volcano. Beth gave the branch a tug.

"Ryan," she hissed, "we're going deeper into the forest."

"I know; what do you want me to do about it? I don't know where we are," Ryan whispered back.

"Haven't you noticed? We've been climbing higher, and look!" She pointed through a clear spot in the trees, at a great dark shape. Council Hill was very close now and blocked out the stars as it loomed over the forest. Ryan gaped at the shadow of the hill. He cleared his throat, and tried to sound important.

"Excuse me... Laughing Cloud? Uh... Are we getting close to shelter, now?"

"Yes, yes... We're very near, just over this ridge."

Ryan shrugged his shoulders and tried to keep pace. Beth sighed. She was miserable. Things seemed as if they could not get any worse. Ryan was worried, too. He knew his mom would be frantic, looking for them everywhere. He had been trusted to take care of Beth. Now, here he was, lost in a forbidden forest, following a strange guide in the middle of the night. Lost in his thoughts, he did not notice when Laughing Cloud suddenly stopped. Ryan let out a grunt as he bumped into him.

"Here we are!" Their guide announced. He turned proudly, grinning.

The ground sloped gently through thinning trees, down to broken boulders at the foot of a studded granite cliff. They were at the base of Council Hill. Laughing Cloud pointed at a great pile of rocks huddled in moonlight, covered with a thatch of branches and reeds. Ryan realized that two large gaps in the rocks were actually a door and window. This was sort of a stone cottage, built right against the bluff. Beth turned to Laughing Cloud.

"You live here?" She craned her neck to look up at him.

"I do," Laughing Cloud said softly, gesturing to the stone house.

"All alone?" Beth looked around for other cottages.

"Yes." His forehead wrinkled in confusion. "Although not always."

The dark window and door surrounded by the quiet boulders beneath the hill looked so forlorn, Beth let out a shuddering sob. The first gust of the storm clattered sticks into the clearing. They rattled like bones. The thought of staying there until morning made her eyes moist. "I want to go back… take me back," she said softly, weeping. She looked up at the tall guide. "Please?"

"Is it that bad?" Laughing Cloud chuckled, looking back at the cottage. "I suppose I'm just used to it now."

"Beth, get a grip." Ryan turned her by the shoulders to look in her face. Her cheeks shone wet in the moonlight. "He's trying to help. It's my fault we got lost."

"I want to go home. I just want to go home, Ryan," she whispered.

"It'll be O.K., We'll get back." He looked up at Laughing Cloud. "Right? You can take us back? To the park, in town?"

"Yes." His dark hair swung around his face as he looked up through the trees. The moon and stars were blotted out again by the clouds. "I have many visitors tonight… these two young ones, and now the storm sits by my door. Don't feel too bad, young Ryan, this forest plays tricks. Sometimes I think the trees get jealous of creatures with legs."

"You don't get lost, do you?" Ryan noted. This made Laughing Cloud burst out with an explosive grunt of laughter.

"These trees are tired of playing with Laughing Cloud. Maybe I am too tall, I think they confuse me for one of them." Big drops of rain began to pock the ground. "Come now. It's time for stories, and unlike trees, I prefer my water from a cup, not on my head." He smiled kindly at the kids, and they followed him down to the curious house in the cliff.

HOME

The lantern flickered as Laughing Cloud hung it from the high ceiling. The rock cabin was larger than it looked from the outside. The front walls were piled stone, fitted tightly together, and secured with mud and clay. The rear was a deep hollow in the face of the cliff, creating a large windowless room. There was a solid wooden door with heavy black hinges inside, bolted in the very back. Everything was neat and clean, if perhaps a little crowded. Colorful and worn blankets lay over sturdy chairs and a small bed in the corner. A heavy table sat in the center of the room with wooden stumps arranged on each side like stools. Bunches of dried leaves, roots, and even whole plants were hanging everywhere. The room was full of a spicy, peppery smell that was pleasant and exciting.

Some of the walls were smooth and painted with bright pictures of animals and people. An amazing depiction of an enormous tree completely covered one wall. It towered as high above the other trees in the forest as a normal tree does over a grass lawn. It was full of animals and birds. Great attention had gone into every tiny detail. Beth was enchanted by the picture, forgetting how upset she was. Drawn to the painting, she reached out her hand to touch it.

"Don't, Beth," Ryan scolded.

24

"It's all right. You can touch it. You won't hurt anything," Laughing Cloud rumbled as he lit another lamp. Beth's fingers touched a brilliant red bird. "I'm glad you like it," he added, squatting beside her on the floor.

"Did you paint this?" Beth asked.

"Yes." He nodded.

"It's… beautiful." She paused as if one word was not enough to describe it.

"I spent a lot of time… But it's still not right. Not like the real one."

"There's a real tree like this?" She turned as Laughing Cloud also raised his hand and gently touched the painted feathers of a bird. Now his face was even with hers, and in the light she could study his features; brown and seamed like old leather, with deep, shining eyes under a dark brow. His mouth was smiling gently, but he seemed sad and thoughtful. He offered her some strips of what looked like dried meat.

"There's no real tree that big, Beth. He's talking about the picture in his mind of what the tree looks like." Ryan took some meat and chewed thoughtfully. It was tough, but tasty, and he realized that he was starving. He tore off another hunk.

"Once there was, a very long time ago." Laughing Cloud rose and pulled up an oaken bucket from a hole in the floor. He ladled water from the bucket into two clay cups, and brought them to Beth and Ryan. It was clear and sweet, but so cold that it made Ryan's head hurt when he gulped it. Laughing Cloud smiled as Ryan grabbed his forehead.

"From the cave spring. Very good water, but you should drink slowly."

"Thanks," Ryan groaned.

"Why do you live way out here?" Beth was still looking at the picture.

"This is my home, where I belong. I have always been here."

"I didn't know anyone lived in these woods."

"Except for ghosts," Ryan added. That made Laughing Cloud laugh and snort.

"No, no. No ghosts. Only me."

"Is it allowed? I mean… don't you have to own this land, this house?" Beth wandered over and sat at the table with Ryan. She grabbed some dried meat and tugged a chunk off with her teeth.

"These rocks were here before me, and they will still be here after I am gone. I do not own any of this, but I am permitted here. This land was for my people, the Oponowa. It was kept for our use only, since the time when Colonel Weston was our friend, many, many years ago."

"Colonel Weston?" Ryan asked, "That's the statue in the park, the goofy guy with the sword."

"Yes. The Oponowa were allies against the British, and our land was respected in thanks. More people came over time, and they took land. Now, we have only this forest, this mountain, which is ancient and sacred."

"But where are the rest of them, the Oponowa?" Beth asked.

"They have gone. Only a few remain, a very few."

"Where did they go? The Oponowa had to go somewhere."

Laughing Cloud shrugged his shoulders. "Many places. They are scattered. Others are here, but not many."

Three figures sat in yellow lamplight, chewing their dinner. Outside, the wind swirled through the trees and lightning flashed. Deep thunder growled and rain swept through the clearing. Laughing Cloud stood and closed the heavy wooden shutters over the window. He turned a chair to face the open door and sat to watch the storm.

The Council Tree

"Was there really a tree like that once?" Beth asked, looking at the wall again.

"Yes. It was the Council Tree. The grandfather of all great trees." Lightning brightened the sky and thunder rolled quickly behind. Sheets of rain washed the rocks in the clearing.

"It's impossible for a tree to grow that big," Ryan said. "It couldn't stand under it's own weight. That thing looks more like a skyscraper." Laughing Cloud turned to him and smiled.

"The name Oponowa means people of the tree, you know," he said softly. "We sing the story of the Council Tree, because it is the story of the Oponowa as well."

He leaned back and shut his eyes. He began to sing softly, a lilting, sad sound. They could not understand the words, but it made Beth think of autumn winds blowing cold and leaves falling into still water. Laughing Cloud sang for only a moment and then sat quietly with his head bowed, his chin resting on his chest.

Ryan nudged Beth under the table. "Is he asleep?" She shrugged her shoulders.

Hearing them, Laughing Cloud opened one eye and grinned. He sat up and scooted his chair around to face them, leaning forward.

"Do you like my song?"

"Yes," the children chimed together. "But I don't understand the words," Beth added.

"Would you like to hear the story?"

"Are you going to fall asleep again?" Ryan teased.

"I'll try to stay awake," Laughing Cloud laughed. "I promise." He leaned back in his chair and turned away from the children, peering out the window and into the darkness. Still looking away, he began to speak in a soft rumble.

"Long ago, when the world was still new and fresh, the Oponowa lived here with many other tribes. There was plenty of game, and everyone was happy. The tribes grew larger and larger. Soon, food was not so easy to find. The tribes began to quarrel with each other over hunting grounds. Then they went to war. It was a bad time. Many people died. Many lodges were burned."

"Among the Oponowa was a great man named Modokana. Even when he walked this earth, my people sang many songs, told many stories about him. Although he was the strongest and bravest of the Oponowa warriors, he hated the battles between the tribes. He wanted peace. He tried to talk to the other warriors, but they would not listen. He even tried to talk to the other tribes, but they thought it was a trick, and beat him. After suffering much, he climbed to the top of Council Hill, and stayed there for fifteen days and nights, praying to the Spirit to bring peace. He ate nothing, and drank only rain and the dew from the grass."

29

"On the fifteenth night, Modokana had no strength left, and he lay on his back, looking at the stars. He watched them turn in the night. He could actually see the great wheel of the sky, rings of stars, dancing in a circle made from millions of silver strands, shining like spider silk. As he watched, one strand fell and dangled just above him. With his last strength, he reached out and caught hold, and it pulled him up, into the sky with the stars."

"There, he met the Great Spirit, and though he was filled with joy and surprise, he did not forget why he came, and he asked the Spirit to bring peace. The Spirit decided to send the Oponowa a great gift, but Modokana was not permitted to return to his people, for once you are taken into the web of the sky, you may never return. Still, Modokana was glad, for he was sure his people would live in peace and happiness." Laughing Cloud rose and pointed out the door. The rain had stopped and the sky was clear, and full of stars.

"There, over that hill, just on the horizon. The brightest star. That is Modokana, where he was placed by the Spirit to watch over his people." Laughing Cloud returned to his chair, and settled heavily, with a sigh.

"Is he really a star?" Beth's eyes were wide.

"It's just a story, Beth." Ryan pointed out the door. "That's probably not even a star. It's Venus or something."

"Modokana had a wife, you know," Laughing Cloud continued. "She was Namino, a beautiful woman. She was the daughter of the Chief, and very clever. We tell many stories about Namino. She worried terribly when Modokana left, but she obeyed him and did not follow. Finally, she could stand it no longer, and she searched for him. She found him on the top of Council Hill, but his spirit had left. Namino wept and tore her hair, but she saw that he wore a smile on his face. As she held him, she found in his fist an acorn. She prepared Modokana and buried him on the hill, watering the acorn with her tears. She slept that night on his grave. She dreamt of her husband, rocking her in his arms."

"When Namino awoke, she was high above the ground, held not by Modokana, but nestled in the limbs of a tree. She carefully climbed down, wondering how she managed to clamber up in her sleep, and saw that the tree had grown overnight from the spot she had laid Modokana. The tree seemed to grow as she watched. It was already as tall as most old trees in the forest. As she made her way back to her lodge and looked back, she could see the first green of its crown rising above the curve of the hill."

"The tree grew and grew, its roots cracked open the hill, and water welled up and ran in rivulets and streams, plummeting in a waterfall over this very same cliff. Where we are right now was once a great pool with water thundering and steaming from high above. The Oponowa were amazed, and moved their village to the top of the hill, under the shelter of the tree."

"Beautiful and strange birds came to roost in the branches of the tree, and their song was the most beautiful of music. Their feathers were long and fine, of all colors, and the Oponowa gathered them. Branches and twigs knocked down by the wind were collected and used for lodge poles or carved into masks, statues and other things. Namino made a staff from a fallen branch. She was growing old, and wanted something to lean on."

"One day, Namino was gathering feathers, feeling lonely. Suddenly she saw a stranger walking under the tree. He wore unusual clothes, and was surprised to see Namino. He babbled in a strange tongue, and he carried a staff like hers.

He gestured towards her, and she saw a beautiful feather in front of her. She picked it up and tucked it into her hair, and when she did, she found she could understand the stranger. Not only could she recognize his speech, she could also understand the birds. For the first time, she could hear the words in their music."

"What did they sing about?" Beth interrupted.

"Oh... About how they loved the spring, and the wind, and how good berries tasted. They sang a lot about how beautiful they thought they were, and how happy they were not to have to creep around in the mud. Silly things mostly. They were pretty, but not very smart."

"Well, who was this stranger?" Ryan asked.

"A chief from another tribe, on the other side of the world, who had been walking under a tree just like the Oponowa's. He'd been thinking how nice it would be to talk to someone, just as Namino had been thinking the same thing. See, this was no ordinary tree. If you've seen a fern that runs roots under the ground to where they burst into another plant... That's how this tree was. Only the roots of this tree ran to the very center of the earth, and popped out all over the world into other great trees."

"That's impossible," Ryan said. "The center of the earth is all melted lava and stuff like that."

"Really?" Laughing Cloud asked. "I didn't know that. Have you seen it?"

"Of course not. How could you get to the center of the earth?"

"Hmmm," Laughing Cloud put his hand on his chin. "I just wondered. You sounded very sure."

"Let him tell the rest of the story," Beth insisted.

"Well, how did they know that there were roots in the center of the earth, and that there were other huge trees?" Ryan tapped his finger on the table.

"From Crow. He told them. He told them about the acorns too."

"A crow told them?"

"Not 'a' crow, 'the' Crow," Laughing Cloud corrected. "Crow had been around a long time, even before people. He was very, very smart, but grumpy, and full of tricks. Sometimes he would help people, and then turn around and get them into trouble. You had to be careful with Crow. The Oponowa didn't know this, and thought him a great friend."

"After Namino had learned she could understand any speech, even the animal's, Crow came and scolded her.

'What good is it to hear, when you can't talk,' he said. 'Pop an acorn in your mouth, and see what happens.' Namino picked up an acorn from the tree, and tried it, but it was too big, and she could only mumble. Crow rolled his eyes. 'Try a smaller one, woman.' She did, and found that she could speak in any language and be understood.

Now, they saw the plan of the Great Spirit. A staff made from this Grandfather Tree would take you into the shade of any of his daughter trees, just by thinking of it. Each tribe made a staff for their Chief, and they would meet under the Council Tree, for that is what they now called it. Can you imagine? Chiefs from hundreds of different tribes, from all over the world, meeting together, speaking and understanding each other. They sat in council, offering advice. They talked through their problems, helped one another, and finally there was peace everywhere."

Laughing Cloud fell silent. He had been gesturing with his hands, leaning forward, eyes shining. Now, he sat back in his chair and rubbed his cheek thoughtfully.

"Well, what happened?" Beth asked insistently.

"Yeah, why did things change?" Ryan leaned on his elbows.

"Because of Crow. But mostly because of Namino's son, Wiakana."

34

CROW'S PLAN

"Wiakana was just a baby when his father fell into the sky. He grew strong and swift, and became a great warrior, with a quick mind like his mother. Even though he was still a young man, he sat with the elders at the Council Tree, and his voice was heard as if he was already a chief. Everyone knew that he would take his Grandfather's place someday as the leader of the Oponowa, but that was not enough for him. Wiakana grew up listening to the deeds of his father, and longed to prove himself. He was too impatient to be very wise, and his heart hungered for more."

"Crow saw all the people were happy, and he was jealous. He was angry at the Great Spirit for presenting such a tremendous gift to the Oponowa, while he received nothing. He decided to take this gift away, but he didn't know how. Crow was patient. He sat, brooding for years. Watching Wiakana, he came up with a plan."

"One day, Wiakana was preparing for a great Council, when Crow flapped up to his shoulder and whispered in his ear.

'Wiakana,' he said. 'Why do you go to the Council, when all they do is bicker and argue?' Wiakana shrugged his shoulders, and Crow fluttered to keep his balance.

'It is the manner in which we keep peace,' he said.

'Well,' Crow responded, 'It seems to me, there are too many chiefs. There should be one great chief to settle things, to make the last argument. That's how your father would have done it.' This pricked Wiakana in his heart, which Crow intended.

'You knew my father?' He asked.

'Of course I did,' said Crow. 'And I can't imagine Modokana putting up with all this wheedling and blabbering. It's a disgrace.' Wiakana began walking to the Council.

'Who would be this great chief?' he asked, and Crow could not help but smile.

'Oh, I don't know. It would have to be the bravest and strongest, someone wise, but young enough to be around for a while… Well, someone like you, actually.'

Wiakana snorted. 'Me? You must be joking. They would never choose someone so young.'

Crow leaned close, right into Wiakana's ear. 'Who says they get to choose?'

Wiakana waved Crow off his shoulder. 'You are too bold, Bird. Get away.'

As Crow flapped off he cried out, 'Modokana was a bold one, boy. They don't sing songs about the timid.'

Wiakana said nothing, but the poison had crept into his mind, and his thoughts were troubled. Crow was right about one thing, the chiefs did argue a lot. Wiakana was tired of hearing it. He felt most of the discussions were silly, and was frustrated when they would not accept his ideas."

"Crow was patient. He waited, and soon Wiakana approached him.

'I have thought about what you said, Crow. How would someone become the great chief?' Crow smiled, and hopped onto Wiakana's shoulder.

'Burn the Council Tree,' he croaked.

'What?!' Wiakana was shocked, but Crow was quick.

'It has served its purpose, the magic is in the staves, the feathers, the acorns, not in the tree. These were the gifts of the Spirit, and you have plenty. More than you will ever need. The tree brought these gifts, but now its job is finished. It grew quickly, and it ages quickly. What will happen when it weakens and rots? The wind will knock it down, and it will smash the Oponowa like ants.'"

"Crow's words played a trick on Wiakana's heart, and although he knew it was wrong, he told himself he would save his people from the danger of the falling tree.

'But how will that make me the great chief?' he asked, and Crow saw that Wiakana had given up pretending that anyone but he would be the great chief.

'The other chiefs are stupid and weak. They take no care where they leave their Council Staves.' Crow sneered.

'Why should they?' Wiakana asked, 'They can always make more.'

'Not when the Tree is gone.' Crow countered. 'Use your staff to visit the other tribes. Borrow each chief's staff, hide them, and then you will have control over the Council. If a chief wants one back, he must agree to make you the great chief.' When Crow said borrow, he meant steal. Wiakana knew it, but he pretended not to. He also knew that Crow's plan was wicked, but he told himself it was the will of the Spirit for him to protect his people from the tree and lead not just the Oponowa, but all the tribes of the world."

"Wiakana still could not think of burning the tree, but he thought he would test Crow's plan. He took his first step down a dark path. He walked to the Council Tree, and using his staff, he visited the other tribes, and found it very easy to 'borrow' the other Council Staves. He slipped quietly in and out of dozens of lodges and huts, tents and caves, gathering the staves and hiding them in his own lodge. Soon he had a great pile, and he admired the cunning simplicity of Crow's plan. Perhaps it would work. He wandered out into the night, to the trunk of the Council Tree, so large that the entire village holding hands could not ring it. Crow saw him and perched on a branch high above, watching."

"Wiakana placed his hand on the solid bark of the tree, hard and rough as stone. He tried to imagine it old and decrepit. He saw it creaking and snapping, pitching slowly and smashing into the village, crushing everyone. He quickly removed flints from his pouch, and with shaking hands, began to strike sparks into the dry moss at the base of the tree. It caught and a small fire crackled as he kneeled."

"He stood and watched the smoke trail up into the leaves, saw the branches swaying, and listened to the birds and wind. He looked away quickly, and stared off into the horizon. There, shining brightly, was Modokana. Wiakana was suddenly filled with shame and fear. He turned and stomped the fire out, burning his feet. His tears sizzled on the hot ground, but he was glad for the pain. He was disgusted and ashamed of himself. He threw his fire stones into the darkness, and ran away, down the hill and into the forest. He never returned, but what happened to him is another story."

"Above, Crow watched him disappear into the night, but he also saw one spark still burning, like a bright berry. He swooped down, carefully fanning it with his wings, and it grew. Suddenly, a bright yellow tongue flicked up through the moss, and crackled quickly up the tree, licking the bark."

"Crow screamed and laughed, and flew up through the branches, very pleased with himself. The tree caught fire immediately, burning as fast as the quickest tinder. Lightning had struck the tree before, and it had never burned, but this was a wicked fire. It was greedy and hungry, and it swept up the tree as fast as a man can run. The beautiful birds were too surprised to even fly away, and squawked horribly as they cooked in their skins. Even Crow was caught as he wheeled around the tree, and found himself engulfed in flames and smoke. Falling through the fire, he choked, and his wings were scorched black. He swooped out and escaped, but the smoke had stolen his voice. Even now, his feathers are black with soot, and he can only cough and screech."

"The Tree groaned and popped. Sap sizzled and boiled out of the trunk. Enormous branches creaked and smashed into the ground. The Oponowa ran from their lodges, but many had already burst into flames. The tree raged like the sun at noon, fire fell all around the village. Everyone ran in terror, some with their hair burning. Many died. All the lodges were burned, including Wiakana's, with all the Council Staves."

"The fire spread to other parts of the forest, and everywhere was heat and smoke, soot and ash. The lucky ones came to this pool at the base of the hill. They waded into the water, watching as the fire gobbled everything."

"The next morning, the fire still smoldered. Everywhere, the earth was scorched and smoking. The Oponowa had wept their tears in the night, and now looked to take care of the injured and rebuild their village. Namino climbed to the top of Council Hill. She still had her staff, and she wanted to find Wiakana, her son. She discovered the fire had burned down into the roots. It had burst out all over the world, consuming the daughter trees also. Crow was right. The traveling magic, the Council magic, was in the staves, but now only a handful of chiefs still had them. Soon, even they stopped meeting."

"Council Hill had become a black, barren rock. A place of death and sadness. The Oponowa moved away, now led by Namino. Where they had once been a happy and playful people, they were now somber and serious. They wore sadness like a scar. The fire had burnt their heart along with the tree. The Oponowa were still the greatest hunters, warriors, and trackers, but became a silent people. They did not dance, and would sing only one song, the song of the Council Tree, so the young ones would never forget."

İnto Council Hill

"You still tell stories, though." Beth smiled at Laughing Cloud.

"Oh, yes. We tell many stories. The Oponowa are excellent at stories." Laughing Cloud stood and stretched, his back popped like twigs snapping.

"Did the Oponowa ever use the magic again?" Beth leaned forward on her stool.

"It's a story, Beth. It's not real. You can't just blip from one place to another. Don't be a baby," Ryan chided.

"Quit acting like you're the boss. I'll believe what I want to. You don't know everything. In fact, I get better grades in school. I know just as much as you do."

"You didn't know how to get out of the forest," Ryan said nastily.

"Neither did you, and you were supposed…"

"You go to the same school?" Laughing Cloud asked. He could see the children were tired, and was trying to stop an ugly fight.

"Yes, only we're off for the summer," Ryan answered.

"Where did you go to school?" Beth asked.

"I learned from the Elders. They told me many stories. I learned from the forest, from the animals."

"How can animals teach you?"

Laughing Cloud reached up and pulled a leather pouch from beneath the rafters. He pulled out a long feather, slightly frayed, but very beautiful.

"I watch them. Sometimes I listen to them."

"Is that a magic feather, from the story? Does it work?" Beth reached out for the feather, and Laughing Cloud handed it to her with a flourish. She ran her fingers along the quill.

"He's pretending. It's just a pretty feather. Right?" Ryan squinted at Laughing Cloud, but he just winked and smiled.

"There are all kinds of magic, Ryan. We are surrounded by it." Laughing Cloud held his arms up. "What makes the moon walk across the night, or the Sun turn in the sky? Isn't that a kind of magic? Have you seen a caterpillar change into a moth? Or wondered what wakes the trees in spring, and paints the forest in fall? I have seen a mother bring a child into the world, and I think it must be a kind of magic too. What is a magic feather compared to that."

"But all those things are ordinary. They happen every day. There's explanations for them. The stories you tell, there's just no way, I mean, animals don't even talk."

"The world is a very big place, full of strange things. The Oponowa knew this. The Council Staff allowed them to see much of it. They found powerful magic, and they brought some things back with them. They became strong, even after the Tree was gone, and the other tribes respected and feared them. Over the generations, all the other peoples had forgotten the great Tree, and the Councils. Only the Oponowa kept the song."

"What kind of magic things did they find?" Beth stifled a yawn.

"You're both tired. You can have my bed. I'll sleep over here. Come on."

Laughing Cloud folded a blanket the children could use for a pillow, and they settled on his mattress. He threw another blanket over them and arranged a spot in the corner for himself. He blew the lamps out and the children heard him settle in. The darkness was deep in the cabin. Insects shrieked and chattered outside. The stone made it cool inside, and they needed their blanket.

Beth was more tired than she had ever been before, but still she could not sleep. Her head was spinning with the story of the Council Tree. She had so many questions. Ryan was anxious as well, worried about his parents looking for them. The bed creaked as he turned, trying to get comfortable. Laughing Cloud sensed his unease.

"Don't worry. A message has already been sent to let your people know you are safe. Sleep."

"When did you do that? You were with us all night." Ryan asked.

"A friend saw us earlier. While we were inside. He knows what to do."

"What did you tell him? I didn't see anybody."

"But he saw you, and there are more ways to send a message than by talking. Sleep, I'll take you home tomorrow."

"Excuse me… Laughing Cloud? How did the Oponowa travel after the tree was gone? What kind of magic did they find in other places?" Beth asked quickly, before he could fall asleep. Laughing Cloud sighed in the darkness.

"I will tell you, and then you must sleep." He was silent for a moment.

"The Councils had stopped, and Namino had gone to join her husband in the sky. She gave her staff to her sister-son, and it was passed on to each chief. The tribe would come here to sing the song of the Council Tree. They gave thanks to the pool that saved the tribe, even after the water dried up. One day the earth shook and rumbled, and a piece of Council Hill cracked, sliding and tumbling away at this very spot. Here, they found a hole in the hill, from the winding roots of the great tree. A twisting cave had been left where the roots had burnt. The cave went deep into the earth and then fell away into a great pit."

The chief of the Oponowa, who still carried Namino's staff, came and explored the cave, to see if he could find another passage. He came back with a magic stone that allowed him to see as far as an eagle sees, and a story of a far away land. He returned to the cave many other times, bringing back more magic things, and strange animals, roots, spices, and other objects. Sometimes he brought only stories. He had this stone house built here, it was called the 'Root House', because of the plants, and because it was the gate into the roots of the earth. A warrior stayed here always, guarding our treasures."

"That stuff is here now?" Ryan interrupted.

"Some. Most of it was stolen. A long time ago."

"Is the cave still there?" Beth whispered.

45

"Of course, it's here. Right here."

"What do you mean here? I didn't see a cave when we came down. Is it hidden?"

"Yes, in a way. It's behind that door in the back. That's the entrance to the cave."

The hair on Ryan's arms stood up. He had always felt uneasy sleeping in a new place, even for a sleep-over at Brad's house. He wasn't very happy that the door at the end of the room opened into a cavern. Even though he knew it was his imagination, he felt that part of the room grow darker. He pulled the blanket to his chin. Beth was a little spooked too, but she also felt excited.

"Do you ever go into it? Where does it lead?"

"He told you before, it goes to a deep pit," Ryan grumped. He preferred not to think about the cave any more than he had to. "I want to sleep." He turned to the wall.

"It was considered a great honor to guard this door," Laughing Cloud said softly. "All the power of the Oponowa was once here in this room. Don't be worried, though. Ryan is right, there is nothing but a deep pit there now. I have answered your questions. Go to sleep now. Good night. I am sorry you were lost, but it's good to tell the story to someone again."

"Thank you, Laughing Cloud," Beth said in the darkness. Ryan stared at the wall. The house was quiet, and eventually even Ryan sank into sleep. Beth was so tired, she didn't even wake up when Ryan snored. She drifted off as Laughing Cloud chanted softly in his sleep, dreaming the song of the stars.

ROOTS OF THE EARTH

Clear, cold air woke Ryan up, and he jumped, not realizing where he was. Birds called to each other and fresh yellow sunlight fell inside the door. Beth lay next to him, still asleep. He remembered, and looked for Laughing Cloud, but the cabin was empty. As he stretched, Beth stirred. She sat up and looked around.

"Where is he?"

"I don't know. Maybe he went for the paper."

She stood up. They were both still dressed from the previous night. "I wonder if he's gone to find help."

"Or some breakfast, hopefully. I'm starving." Ryan's stomach was growling. "He's got to have some food around here somewhere."

"You want to try eating this?" Beth tugged at a bunch of long brown leaves hanging from the rafters. "The way he talked last night, you'd probably end up a squirrel or something."

"There's regular food here, I know it. Even that dried meat stuff would work. I'm starving." Ryan began to poke through the shelves and bins around the room.

47

"I don't know if I'd do that. Some of this stuff is pretty weird."

"Quit worrying, and help me find something to eat. Look over there, where he pulled down that pouch. Maybe he's got some food stashed there."

Beth climbed on the table to reach the rafters. She pulled down several pouches. There were feathers, and acorns, small colored stones, and something that looked like ashes or dust, but no food. She held an acorn in her hand.

"Ryan, do you believe the story he told us last night?"

"No. No way. It's just a story. You've heard stories like that. Everybody has some kind of legend; Greeks, Romans, Indians, whatever."

"You don't think even part of it is true?"

Ryan was on his hands and knees, looking under a table at some rough clay jars. His voice was hollow. "Maybe, but what's the difference?"

"I dreamed about it all last night. What do you think the cave is like?"

"Aha! Here we go." He reached into the jars and pulled out some dried meat and what looked like hard biscuits. "There's little dried berry-looking things, but I don't know if I want to try those." Ryan stuck a handful in his pocket, and kept looking. Beth stashed the acorn she was holding in her overalls, and pulled out the pouch with the feathers. They were all different sizes and colors, and she picked a short one that she was sure Laughing Cloud wouldn't miss.

"Put that stuff back," Ryan warned.

"Don't tell me what to do. Look how many he has. He won't mind. I just want to see if it's true or not. I'd ask him if he was here."

"That's stealing and you know it." Ryan munched on the dried meat.

"Look at you. What about the food you're eating?"

"That's different. We've got to eat."

"It probably wouldn't kill you if you skipped breakfast. Maybe that's all he has, and you're gobbling it up. Here, let me have some too." She snatched a piece from Ryan.

Beth hopped down from the table and wandered over to the door on the far wall, still chewing. "There's no lock," she noted, touching the heavy, wooden handle.

"Don't, Beth. He might have it rigged or something. He said they used to guard it close."

"I'll open it slowly." She pulled lightly, and the door did not budge.

"Quit it, Beth. We'll ask him when he comes back. If you make him mad, he might not take us home."

"He's not like that. If he didn't want us going in, he would have said something before." She pulled harder, but the door still didn't budge. "You really don't want to know what's behind here? Come on and help me." Now she had all her weight behind her as she tugged. Ryan moved behind her to help. With a screech, the door flew open. Beth fell backwards, knocking Ryan down. They both tumbled into a heap as the heavy door banged against the wall.

Behind the door and frame, a rough passage had been hewn out of the rock. It was a dark hole, wide enough for the kids, but a large adult would have to squeeze through. Cool air bellowed from the cave, with a musty smell. Beth untangled herself from Ryan. She found one of the lamps and lit it.

"He crawls through that?" Ryan gasped

"Maybe it gets bigger, further in." Beth said, walking over to the entrance and peering in with the lamp. "Look, it does, I can see it open into a room, just a few feet in."

"I'm not going in there. No way."

"Oh, are you scared? What's wrong, Ryan? Who's the baby, now? I'm going to see what's in there. You can hide under the blankets if you want."

"C'mon, Beth, you don't know anything about caves. You can't…"

"You don't know anything either," she interrupted. "Are you coming or not?"

Ryan shrugged his shoulders and grabbed the other lamp. "I can't let you go in there alone. We'll take a look and then come back out."

The two crept cautiously into the cave. Beth was right. The passage led to a circular room, large enough to stand in. There were baskets and pouches along the walls, and Ryan could smell apples.

"He must use this like a root cellar. I bet most of his food is in here."

"Look!" Beth pointed to the far end of the room. Another smooth tunnel, much larger than the first, bent away into darkness. Beth hurried over and peered around the corner. Ryan followed her, stumbling on something that clattered away just outside the flickering light. Raising the lamp, he saw a length of pale wood, carved and twisted, laying on the stone. Beth saw it too, and came back into the room as Ryan picked it up. It was smooth and silvery, except where it had been carved. The wood was springy and fresh, as if it had just been cut, but the carvings were worn. The top had images of leaves and birds whittled into the wood, and the base was covered in twisting roots and vines, wound around an object that looked like a heart or a face, it was hard to tell. The wood in the middle was fresh, and light, and felt good to hold.

"It's the staff. It must be," Beth said slowly.

"It's a walking stick. He probably uses it in this cave, or on his walks. It's good to have something like this to help you get out of a hole, or just to prop up on. Let's go back now."

"Let's go a little further. I want to see this pit."

"You might see it up close when you fall down into it."

"Ryan, we are never going to get to come here again. Let's have a look."

"Fine, but let me go in front. I'll use the stick to feel for holes. I don't trust this cave."

Beth nodded, and they moved down the passage, cautiously. They could stand in this cavern, and as they walked on, the tunnel continued to grow wider. White streaks of glittering minerals painted the walls. As they moved deeper into the hill, thin strands of sparkling crystals dripped from the ceiling. The lantern light reflected bands of color from prisms in the passageway. They looked around in wonder, forgetting their caution. The walls moved away, and before them a dark abyss opened in the floor. Above in the roof, a thousand shining white daggers glistened.

"Wow!" Beth gasped, looking at the enormous chasm in the ground. Ryan tossed a pebble from the floor and listened for it to hit. There was silence.

"End of the line. Now, can we go back?" Beth nodded.

"Do you think there's a bottom?"

"There has to be. It looks pretty deep, though. This is some cave. I don't know how they managed to keep it a secret. They should have tours and stuff."

"It'd be a pretty short tour."

"I don't know, how long did it take us to get this far?"

"I'm not wearing a watch, I don't know." She shrugged her shoulders, and Ryan realized he wasn't sure how long they had been either.

"If L.C. comes back, he'll think we left."

"L.C..? Oh..." Beth smiled. "No. We left the door open. He'll figure it out."

"I hope he's not mad. Let's hurry back." Beth and Ryan moved quicker down the passage as it narrowed. Ryan rapped his stick on the stone. They followed the winding tunnel around a bend, and stopped suddenly. Just inside the lamplight they now saw two dark passageways.

Winding Caverns

Ryan remembered his father's advice about paths again. He noted that apparently, caves are even trickier than trails. As you follow one cavern, another may open up behind you. He wished he had been more careful and noticed the new passage, or marked the way back to the surface. Beth and Ryan had never been in a cave, and they had been too busy looking out for pits and staring at pretty rock formations. Now they had to choose.

"Great!" Ryan shouted, his voice echoing through the caverns. "You got us lost again!"

"I got us lost? You were in front, tapping around for traps like an idiot. You were supposed to be paying attention to where we were going. Don't blame me, Ryan."

"Whose idea was it to even come down here in the first place?"

"Ryan, what difference does it make? It's not going to help us find a way back."

"Well, which one is it?"

"The one on the left, I think. It seems larger."

"Are you sure? Look at that crumbled spot on the right one, that looks kind of familiar, I noticed it right as the passage widened up."

"No, I think it's the left. See that shiny spot? I remember that. It's the left."

"You were sure in the forest too."

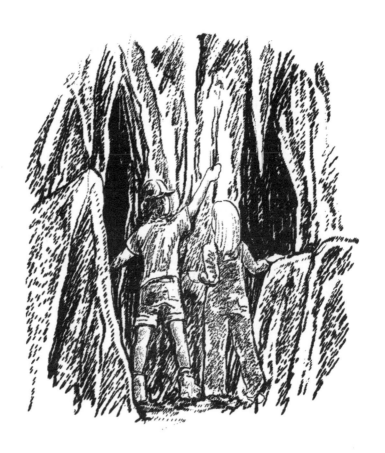

"Well, you decide then, if you're so smart." Beth crossed her arms, exasperated.

Ryan looked from one to another, back and forth, while Beth tapped her foot. Finally he threw his hands up.

"I can't. They both look familiar. Here. Let's let the stick decide." He held the stick up in front of him, between his thumb and forefinger. "O.K. stick. Tell us where we need to go." Balancing the base gently on the stone, he closed his eyes and let go. Clattering echoes bounced around the cavern. The stick pointed to the left. He took his spot in front again. "Let's go. We've been in here too long already."

They came to more intersections as they continued, and they used the stick again. Ryan was sure they were hopelessly lost, Beth was too, but wouldn't say so, because she felt like it was her fault. Beth's lamp had run out of oil, and Ryan's felt light. They were both very frightened, as the darkness crowded around them. Ryan had just decided to turn back and try another way, when he felt air stir on his face.

"Did you feel that?" He asked Beth.

"Yes, and it feels a little warmer, too." Ryan noted. His lamp began to flicker, and he felt sick in his stomach as the darkness crept closer. The passage became smoother and narrower, but continued uphill. The lamp sputtered and went out. In the pitch black, he heard Beth groan.

"It's all right, Beth. Just move to the wall. I think we're close, we can feel our way out. Hang on to my shirt." Ryan put his right hand against the wall, and used the staff to tap in front of him. They were still climbing, the walls opened up, and the sounds of their feet echoed. The sides of the passage felt rough and crumbling. Several times he stumbled over breakdown in his path, but he struggled on. Wiping his face and forehead, he tasted salt, but not from his sweat. It was on his hand. It was covered in salt. He could smell it now in the walls. A few steps later, it seemed that the darkness was a little brighter. Suddenly, light flooded them as they squeezed behind a large boulder. What appeared to be an enormous doorway leaked sunlight, illuminating a huge cavern the size of a cathedral. The walls were gouged, and chunks of mineral salt lay all over the floor.

As their eyes adjusted, they saw the light was shining from between two massive stone doors, taller than a house.

"O.K. how do we get out?" Beth asked, swinging her lamp. Even though they were still lost, she felt happy just to be out of the dark.

"Through these doors, I guess." He walked across the room and pounded on one of the great slabs. His hand made a flat slap against the stone. "Ow! This is not going to be easy. Look around and see if you can find another place to get out." Beth wandered around the edge of the room, searching for another entrance. Ryan peeped through the space between the doors and felt warm air. He could only see green bushes and trees, and a low gray wall of stone.

"What do you see?" Beth asked from across the cavern.

"Nothing. A forest maybe. I can't tell. We're probably on the other side of the hill. This must be an old salt mine or something"

"I think that's the only way out. I don't see any other doors." Beth walked back towards Ryan. "We have to get these open."

"No way. They're huge. I can't even budge them. You need a bulldozer to get these things open."

"We've got to try, at least. Come on. Maybe they're on special hinges or something." Beth turned and put her back to the door. "Ready? On three. One.. Two... Push!" They both groaned and grunted as they shoved the door, but their feet just slipped on the dirt. Soon they both collapsed on the ground, frustrated. Ryan kicked the door.

"Open up! Open!" He kicked it again, too hard, and hurt his foot. He hopped around on the other foot, angry and muttering. He picked up the stick and banged it against the door.

"Don't! You'll break it! Ryan!" But he was in pain and too angry to listen. He smacked the staff against the doors and screamed.

"Open! Stupid doors! Open up!" Sparks flew off the head of the staff as he pounded the stone. Ryan fell back in a heap as both doors gave a piercing screech, grinding stone as they threw themselves wide, smacking against the door frame with a great boom that tore them off their hinges. They collapsed, thundering to the ground in clouds of dust and debris.

Deafened by the destruction, Beth and Ryan coughed and squinted against the sunlight pouring in. The doors lay ruined and silent, but the thunder continued. The ground rumbled and the air shook. Everywhere was a blaring that made their ears ring. Blinking and covered in dust, they stumbled into the courtyard in front of the cave, just as dozens of elephants stampeded up the hill.

Gandhar

Stunned, Beth grabbed Ryan as the ground trembled. Great gray beasts marched into the ruined plaza of stone before the cave. There were too many to count, piling in from stone ramps on both sides of the hill. The wrinkled giants slowed to a walk as they saw the children and stopped, nodding and swinging their trunks. Ryan held his staff up defensively, and Beth looked for something to protect herself with. Her left hand found the feather in her pocket. That was all she had. She bent and picked up a hefty rock. It was useless of course, the tiniest of the elephants could have trampled both of them in two seconds.

An elephant nudged through the crowd and approached the children. He didn't walk directly to them, but sidled up slowly, nervously, stopping about ten feet away.

"Who are you?" the elephant said, in a deep, nasal voice, like someone with a bad cold. Beth dropped the rock in astonishment.

"I'm.. I'm Beth Cooper. This is my cousin, Ryan." The elephant gave no indication he understood. He was close enough that Beth felt the air stir as he flapped his ears.

"Who are you talking to?" Ryan hissed, keeping an eye on the elephant.

"Didn't you hear him? He asked who we are."

"Who are you?" The elephant repeated, shifting his weight to another foot and looking irritated.

"There! He asked again." Beth said, and turned back to the beast. She raised her voice slightly and said carefully, "I'm Beth Cooper, and…" Just then, she noticed that she had Laughing Cloud's feather still clutched in her hand. She paused and placed it in her hair. Reaching into her pocket, she drew out the small brown acorn and popped it into her mouth.

"I'm Be'h Coope' an' thish ish ma cousin, Rya'," she warbled. It wasn't easy to talk with an acorn in her mouth. The elephant stepped half a pace back, and nodded it's great head.

"You understand speech, good. I was afraid that you were demons. I am Gandhar, Be'h Coope'. The herd bids you welcome."

"It's just Beth," she said, rolling the acorn in her mouth where it was out of the way. It made her cheek bulge. "This is Ryan," she added

"What's he got to say?" Ryan poked her in the arm. "All I can hear is wheezing and gurgling."

"He's Gandhar, and he says hello."

"They should call him Pinky, with all those spots. Ask him where we are."

"Gandhar, where is this place?" Beth asked.

"We are at the cave of elephants, in the ruined city of Panagati." Beth relayed this to Ryan.

"That doesn't help much. Ask him what country we're in." Ryan lowered his staff, shaking dust out of his hair.

"Gandhar, tell us whose country this is, the name of this land." Beth moved slightly closer to the baggy giant.

"Hmmm. This was once called the Partha forest, long ago, by creatures like yourself. But they have long gone. Now this land is ruled by my grandmother, Madriva, the head of my clan." As Gandhar finished, Beth noticed that several elephants had inched forward. She thought they were trying to listen to the conversation, but then she saw that many had their trunks up and were snuffling loudly in the direction of the cave.

"What are they doing?" Beth asked Gandhar.

"This was once our cave… for the salt, you understand. These doors have been locked for many years now. This cave was once opened just for my clan, for us to have access to the salt. The people here once gave great reverence to us, and we were friends. They knew that we need the mineral to survive. There are only a few other places we can find salt. That is why we hurried up here. All of us are pleased the doors have been knocked down forever. We are thankful that you have used your magic to return it to us. I am your servant." As he said this, Gandhar bowed on one knee, touching his forehead to the ground. The other elephants, seeing him, did likewise. Beth and Ryan stood in a semi-circle of bowing elephants and looked at each other, utterly confused.

"I was wondering," Gandhar said as he rose, almost timidly. "Would you mind if we went into the cave now?"

"Of course not," Beth answered. She had hardly spoken, when Gandhar turned and swayed into the dark hole. The other elephants crowded and jostled behind him, keeping a respectful distance from the children. They scooped up hunks of the salt, grinding and crunching. They scored the walls with their tusks, gouging out more salt, and let out echoing trumpet blasts. Beth and Ryan hurried away from the entrance to the low stone wall where it was quieter. There they stood high over a plain of stone, a large city now choked with jungle. The lush tangle of trees, full of strange hoots and shrieking, stretched to the horizon.

"Where are we?" Beth whispered sadly. "How did this happen?"

"Somewhere close to the equator, as hot as it is," Ryan said, wiping his forehead.

"I just want to be home. The harder we try, the further away we seem to get." Beth's breath hitched in her chest. "How are we ever going to get back?"

"I don't know. I couldn't tell you how we got here. But we should start by figuring out where we are. I think it must be Africa. Look at the jungle, the elephants…"

"No," Beth replied. "These aren't African elephants. They're Indian elephants.

"How do you know?" Ryan twirled the staff.

"Because I pay attention. These are smaller, and their ears don't stick out like sails. Their heads are a different shape too. Haven't you been to a zoo?" She rolled her eyes at Ryan.

"Fine… So we're in India."

"Maybe. It could be a thousand different places in Asia."

"But there were people here once. They've got to be around somewhere. We get Pinky to take us to them, and then they'll help us get home. All we need to find is a phone."

"His name is Gandhar."

"Whatever, you said he owes us for opening that cave."

"It seems so. How did you do that, anyway?"

"I'm not sure," Ryan answered, looking affectionately at the staff. "I guess this old stick still has some bang."

"So all of L.C.'s stories are true, after all," Beth whispered. "The Council Tree, the staff, the feather, the acorn, all of it. He was telling us the truth the whole time." Beth looked at Ryan. Ryan opened his mouth to respond, but before he could, they felt massive footfalls behind them.

MARCH TO THE SHRINE

Gandhar approached the children, saluting them with a wave of his trunk.

"Much better. It's been many years since I tasted the salt in that cave."

"Why didn't you just knock the doors down?" Ryan asked, and Beth interpreted, craning her neck to look up at the elephant.

"Oh… It's not that easy. Those weren't ordinary doors. It's not just that they were big and heavy. We might have managed that, but they were locked with magic by the demon, Saudaheva."

"A real demon? Is he still here?" Beth sat on the wall across from Gandhar.

"He hasn't been here for many years. He had a quarrel with my grandsire. He wanted all the bull elephants to help him fight the Old Maharajah, and made us many promises. My grandsire didn't trust him and refused, so he locked this cave to punish us. That was before he became a demon, while he still walked and talked like a real man. He spent a lot of time in this cave, about his dark business. He wiggled into the bowels of this mountain like a worm, stealing the secrets from its heart. Now Saudaheva has been twisted by his sorcery. He has learned how to become a hideous tiger, and spends most of his time in that shape, stalking the jungle."

"How do you know if it's a real tiger or Saudaheva?" Ryan asked. Gandhar shifted his weight and flapped his ears, the elephant equivalent of shrugging his shoulders.

"I don't believe anyone's gotten a good look at him. If you do, that's the last thing you'll see. He's an evil demon, no doubt. Now the Old Maharajah is dead. Things are not good for your kind."

"There are people here? Is there a town or something nearby?" Beth got up from the stone wall, hopeful.

"There is a great city, but not close. It is on the Vasus river, many days away. That land is called Rhamanapore, and we do not belong there. Elephants are taken and made to be slaves, not like here in Panagati, where we worked together as friends. That was long ago. My Grandmother, Madriva, knows of those times."

"Can you take us there? We need to find other people, to help us get back," Beth pleaded. Gandhar looked at her, puzzled.

"Why don't you just go back the same way you came?"

"It doesn't work like that, we can't find our way. We need help to get home," Beth told Ghandar as Ryan looked back at the dark cave. Gandhar turned too, and shook his head.

"You are strange sorcerers. You have the power to break open mountains, but cannot find your way back, or even summon help. Very strange, but then, your kind have always been strange. A very forgetful herd. Look at this city, no man even remembers it. Once a great and mighty nation prospered, a nation we were a part of. The elephants still remember. We still abide by our promises. But man? Where is he? They capture and beat us, kill us for our tusks and hide." Gandhar stopped and sighed, it sounded like a burst of air through a garden hose. "It was not always so. Of course we will help you, but I cannot take you to Rhamanapore just yet. I am to meet my Grandmother at the shrine of Lord Ganesh, not far from here. She will advise us what to do." Gandhar turned and called to one of the younger elephants, who turned and bounded over to the children, shaking seed pods from the tree above them.

"This is my nephew, Vati. He will bear Ryan, and you may ride on me." Gandhar stooped low, offering his front leg as a step. Vati quickly did the same as his uncle. Ryan and Beth stood frozen in their places.

"Come now," Gandhar said. "I insist. It is no shame for me to carry you, please do not worry on my account. The others have seen your powers, and will understand. We cannot delay much longer, or I will be late. It is not advisable to keep my Grandmother waiting."

Beth was first. She had grown to like Gandhar from talking to him. Ryan was more cautious. He had not been able to understand their speech like Beth, and Vati looked like a healthy, energetic brute. Beth clambered up, clinging to the loose, rough hide. She got her foot on the base of Gandhar's ear, right next to his skull, and swung up and across his neck. Ryan had more trouble. Vati had not knelt quite as low, and was larger than Gandhar. Ryan was also trying to hold on to his staff, and the base of the stick was waving close to Vati's eye. Vati turned his head skittishly and Ryan was dumped on the ground. Beth laughed so hard she thought she was going to fall as well. Gandhar stood and she swayed as he nudged Vati with his trunk.

"Be gentle, nephew, or I will teach you better." Gandhar threatened. Vati knelt again. Ryan handed the staff up to Beth and he scrambled onto Vati's neck. She handed the stick back as Vati stood and the elephants moved toward the stone ramp. Gandhar gave a great blast and Beth's ears rang as she clapped her hands to her head. Ryan turned to see the other gray beasts form up behind Gandhar and Vati, shuffling in a great mass of ears and tusks.

It was wonderful to ride, Beth thought. She sat high, rocking and swaying as Gandhar plodded down the ramp toward the ruined streets of Panagati. She felt like she was flying, descending into the ancient city, bobbing on a giant gray bird.

Ryan was not having as much fun. He was clinging onto Vati's neck with his hands instead of using his legs. Vati had much more energy than his old uncle, and bounced Ryan vigorously as they went down the ramp. At the base, two giant carved statues rose on either side. The figure had deteriorated, but Beth could see it was like a man, with an elephant's head and trunk, and four arms.

"Lord Ganesh," Gandhar said, sensing her interest. "The son of Shiva and Parvathi. He was given an elephant's head and was venerated for his wisdom and knowledge. This city was founded by him, and our clan was welcomed and revered."

He made his way down a once broad avenue, now gripped by trees and vines. Crumbling stone walls lined the street, covered in elaborate carvings. As they worked their way down the cracked lane, Beth's eyes fell on a large temple just ahead.

"Look Ryan!" she shouted, pointing. He glanced in her direction. There on the wall, a great tree was carved, in a

different style, but remarkably similar to the one in the stone cabin. "What is that, Gandhar?" She asked excitedly.

"Mmmm… My Grandmother would know better, but I remember she told me a story once of the giant Banyan Tree. It spread over the city, and gave protection to all. It was eaten by a fire demon in the night. The people fled, and the city never recovered. These people had many stories. Now, they have all been eaten by the jungle."

Beth saw a great dark root had split the granite carving of the tree, cracking the stone. They swayed on, coming to the giant tumbled gates of the city. The elephants picked their way through the fallen blocks and the jungle closed around them.

Madriva

Beneath the canopy of the trees, it was difficult to tell what time it was. Beth stared at the back of Gandhar's head, swaying for what seemed like hours. It was hot, damp, and suffocating in the dense jungle, and Beth waved at the cloud of insects around her head. They bit her face and arms, swarming around her eyes.

"These bugs are awful!" She shouted, flailing her hands around her head.

"Here, use this." Ghandar snapped off a bushy twig with his trunk and handed it back. "You get used to them. Of course, my skin is a lot thicker too."

"I can't imagine getting used to this, ever!" Beth fanned her face. A thumping and crashing made her turn. Vati rushed ahead and then circled back to his friends. Ryan was tossed like a ship in a storm.

"Let's trade!" he shouted as Vati stomped ahead of Gandhar. He was starting to get used to the ride, but looked at Beth on the gentle, plodding Gandhar with envy. Vati was not used to having a rider and let branches brush his back, smacking into Ryan.

"Hey!" he complained, using the staff to knock the limbs away. "Watch it, will'ya?" But Ryan was without an acorn, and Vati could not understand him. The younger elephant ripped down another branch with his trunk and used it to swat flies. Occasionally he would swipe Ryan with it, and Beth was unsure if it was by accident or not.

They came to a clearing, and the path turned into cracked stone. The jungle faded back like curtains, unveiling an enormous temple rising into the sky. Tier after tier of carved stone figures held each other up. Slowly crumbling, dark holes gaped where faces once smiled and grimaced. The carvings were stacked high, holding up a giant lotus flower at the tower's pinnacle, petals spread above the forest canopy. They passed through a great arch in a thick wall and into a courtyard. They could finally see the late afternoon sky, reddening into dusk. Several elephants wandered around the base of the temple beneath another grand statue of Lord Ganesh.

There in the center of a small group was the most ancient elephant either child had ever seen. Her skin was baggy and loose, hanging off the sides of her body. Her lower lip and ears drooped. Beth could see the outline of her ribs and the sharp bones of her hips and back poking up just beneath her skin.

"You are late, Gandhar," she croaked as they approached.

"My apologies, Grandmother. It has been an eventful day. The salt cave at Panagati is open again. The doors have been smashed forever."

"Who do you bear on your back? Draw nearer, where I may see." Gandhar approached, with Vati hiding behind him, not quite as bold as he had been. Gandhar knelt and Beth dismounted. Ryan did likewise. Beth's legs felt strange after sitting on an elephant so long, as if she were on a boat all day.

"These are the sorcerers who have destroyed the gates of the salt cave. Beth, Ryan, please know you are in the presence of Madriva, Grand Matriarch of the Herd, Eldest Matron of our Clan." Both children bowed their heads.

"That's your excuse for being late? Hmmph. I suppose they want something. Humans always want something."

"They wish to go to Rhamanapore."

"So they shall. Off with them, then. Good-bye."

"They have asked that we take them."

"Certainly not. Strange things are afoot in that troubled kingdom. That awful Saudaheva is running things now, so I'm told, and I'll have nothing to do with it."

"Surely the new Maharaja will…"

"The new Maharaja is a fool. He has been swayed by Saudaheva and he will be dead soon, if he is not already. Those humans are good for nothing. They have stolen our brethren, killed our sisters, and were a constant source of trouble to my dear husband."

"Please, Ma'am, we don't have any other way to get home," Beth piped up. Gandhar turned his head and looked at her severely. Madriva paused, as if she had noticed Beth for the first time.

"So… This one speaks. Well, little human, why don't you use your magic to get home? An enchantress like you shouldn't need help from an old cow like me, eh?"

"Please. We opened the doors. Can't you just do this one favor for us?"

"I never asked you to do anything. If you smashed the silly doors it was your own doing. I owe you nothing. I don't know what my Grandson has promised you. He is a hasty lad. If you wish to get home, you'll need to find something better to offer than that."

"What do you want? We'll help you any way we can."

"Yes… That's more like it. It so happens that I do have a task for you. Nothing too taxing. Certainly within the abilities of a great magician such as yourself." She turned to one of the elephants beside her. "Bring the boy!" she commanded. The attending elephant scuttled away into the dark recesses of the temple. Ryan nudged Beth and she quickly told him what was happening as well as she could, but stopped short as Madriva began again.

"You see, humans have been cropping up like weeds lately. Why, only a week ago, I went to take my bath in a nice hidden pool, when there I found this boy, broken and bleeding. We have cared for him, as best we could, and he is fit to travel now. So take him and be gone."

"Why did she save him?" Ryan asked, and Beth translated.

"Because we promised," She said fiercely, her eyes blazing. "Long before I was born, we promised not to harm humans, or allow them to be harmed. It was a pact, between us. We have remembered and kept our promise. Humans have not. You have even forgotten how to talk to us. But this boy is different, he remembers our speech, and that means he is from an ancient and noble family. Now take the boy and go. I will send Gandhar and Vati to bear you as far as the common road. Then you must continue as you can. Here."

From the mouth of the temple came a boy about Beth's age. He was skinny and bruised, and wore tattered clothing. Beth saw the rags were stained with blood in several spots. Even at a distance, she noticed fresh cuts on his face and arms, just starting to heal. His black hair was long and unkempt, and his eyes looked huge in his drawn face. Despite his pitiful condition, he grinned at them. Putting his palms together he bowed to Madriva.

"Thank you for your mercies, Madriva. You have saved my miserable life, and I will try to be worthy of this gift. I have heard your command to leave and will obey. Know that I will always remember your kindness, and honor you and your clan."

Beth looked at the bedraggled boy in surprise. His manner and speech did not fit with his terrible condition. He turned to Beth and Ryan.

"Hello! You look young to be magicians, or is that part of your magic?" the boy said, laughing. "I am Drishad. I am pleased we are to be traveling companions. But I must know before we leave, where did you find those clothes?"

"Can you understand him?" Ryan whispered to Beth.

"Yep. He says you look funny." The boy grinned wider as he realized that Beth understood him.

"I meant nothing, I assure you. I have one sorcerer after me already. I certainly don't need to be out of favor with two more."

"We aren't magicians. I'm Beth and this is my cousin, Ryan. We're just ordinary people. No different than you," Beth said, smiling back.

"Aha!" Drishad said. "But how do you know I am ordinary?"

"Why'd you tell him that? It might have been useful for him to think we knew magic," Ryan mumbled, nudging Beth.

"Enough. It is time for you to go," Madriva commanded. "You have a few hours of daylight left, and I want you away from here. I don't like surprises. There is sorcery here, and that can only mean Saudaheva is involved somehow. I have been annoyed enough, and I have other matters to attend to. Gandhar, Vati, take charge of the humans." Madriva waved her trunk in dismissal and slowly moved toward the temple entrance, surrounded by her attendants.

Ryan and Beth clambered aboard the broad backs of the two elephants. Drishad hopped up behind Beth on Gandhar. He was nimble and quick, and seemed very familiar with travel by elephant. Ryan was groaning and grumbling as Vati rose. Both animals trundled out the archway and toward the jungle road.

DRISHAD

"I'm tired of not being able to understand what anybody is saying!" Ryan grumped. "You chatter away with everybody, and I can only understand you. It's like listening to you talk on the phone."

"You decided not to bring a feather, remember? You didn't believe they worked. You said it was stealing."

"It is stealing. It's wrong. I was just trying to do what's right."

"Really? how about that staff? Where did that come from, exactly?"

Drishad just watched them both with big eyes. He could only understand Beth, but he could tell they were arguing.

"What feather?" he asked.

"Here." Beth pulled the feather from her hair and handed it to Drishad. "I'm tired of listening to him anyway. You can have a turn."

"It isn't really fair," Ryan said to Drishad. "I can't understand what anyone is saying, and I don't think Beth is really telling me everything that's going on. It's like… Blah, blah, blah… get on an elephant. Blah, blah, blah… get off…

get back on again. I'm tired of it. I just want to get home, where everything is normal."

Drishad gripped the feather tightly and tried to answer him, but he didn't have the acorn, and Ryan couldn't understand his language. Drishad tried to talk to Beth, but she couldn't comprehend him either without the feather. He handed it back to her.

"Maybe it is better if you keep your magic. It makes me nervous. Magic has not been kind to my family."

"Who is your family? Where are you from?" Beth turned to look at him over her shoulder.

"I am of Rhamanapore, from the Karhada palace."

"Hey, Ryan! Drishad is from Rhamanapore, maybe he can help us." She turned back to her new friend. "Do you have a place where we could use the phone? Make a couple of calls? Can you find your way back there?"

Drishad looked at her in bewilderment and sadness. "I cannot go back. Ever. I am trying to get away. I'm sorry. I would like to help. And I do not know what this 'phone' is… Perhaps we have a different word. Describe it, tell me what it does."

"It's a phone, Drishad. You know… Ring, ring… you pick it up, talk into it." She held her thumb and pinky to her ear, like a handset. "Hello? Who is it? You know… A phone, Drishad. Tel-e-phone." She sounded out the syllables, but Drishad just looked at her blankly.

"Who do you speak to? Gods? Devils?"

"No, no," Beth sighed, frustrated. "You talk to whoever is on the other end. Friends, your parents…" At the thought of her folks, she fell quiet and looked straight ahead into the dark trees.

"I'm sorry. This is powerful magic. We do not have this phone in Rhamanapore.

"He doesn't know what a phone is," Beth said to Ryan. "He says they don't have one in the country."

"Maybe they're too poor to afford one. Lots of places still don't have phones. Ask him if he's seen one at this palace place," Ryan said, and Beth translated. Drishad shook his head.

"I did not know of one while I was at the palace. Although, they may have something like it now. But you would not want to use anything there. It is a cursed place - a wicked, ugly place."

"What were you doing there, then?"

"It was my home once. My grandfather was the Maharajah. I was once a prince, although I can hardly remember anything about it. I have only known that palace as I left it: a dark and hideous fortress, stinking of death and evil."

"He says he was a prince." Beth relayed to Ryan.

"He doesn't look like a prince. He's probably making it up. I think a prince would know what a phone is. He probably was a servant or something in the palace."

"How do I know you aren't lying?" Beth asked Drishad, and was sorry she had said it so bluntly. A look of pain and shock crossed his face, replaced quickly with anger.

"Why would I lie about being under a curse? Would you lie about your grandfather being poisoned? Or lie about watching your uncle be enchanted and betray his people? Would you lie about seeing your entire family murdered, your country destroyed? Would you lie about being enslaved by a demon, living as a worm crushed beneath his foot, or about fleeing into an unknown wilderness, chased by creatures that only live in your worst dreams?" Drishad's face turned pale, and his anger failed him. Tears welled in his eyes, and he buried his face in his hands. Looking up desperately, he swung his legs over Gandhar's side, and dropped to the ground. He disappeared into the hooting jungle faster than Gandhar could stop and turn his head.

"Jeez, Beth, what'd you say to him?" Ryan asked, raising an eyebrow.

"I'm sorry!" Beth shouted into the ferns that swished behind Drishad. "I believe you! I'm sorry!"

Gandhar shouldered through the trees, pounding into the darkening jungle. Beth lay face down on his back, to keep the branches from brushing her off. Gandhar muttered and griped about troublesome humans as he trundled at a surprising pace through the dense foliage. He stopped suddenly, and Beth swayed as he jerked his head sharply to the left. She looked up as she heard Drishad shout. Gandhar's trunk was wrapped around the boy's waist, and he was lifted from his hiding spot behind a rotted log. Drishad's face was still contorted with fear and weeping, and he struggled with the elephant's grip.

"Enough!" Gandhar boomed, sounding a lot like his grandmother. "Be still, or I will shake you into a more passive mood."

Drishad calmed immediately and Gandhar placed him on the ground. Silently, he climbed back aboard the elephant, and Gandhar returned to the path. Drishad kept his head down, and would not look at Beth. Vati was pacing impatiently as they returned.

"What happened?" Ryan asked, but Beth ignored him.

They marched in silence for some time as it grew darker. Gandhar kept muttering under his breath.

"What are you grumbling about?" Beth asked, eager to talk to someone.

"This little task has kept me from other duties, Beth Cooper. I do not mind helping you, but I had other business with Madriva, and now she has sent me on this errand before I could resolve it."

"Why didn't you tell her that when you had the chance?" Beth asked, waving at the insects with her wand of leaves.

"One does not question the Matriarch, no matter what her decision. It is our way.. I wouldn't expect you to understand. Humans are always setting up one king after another. Very disruptive. The strength of the clan depends on the strength of the Matron." Ghandar huffed.

"Well. I come from a place where we don't have kings or Matrons or any royalty at all." Beth said, with equal disdain.

"How horrid. I imagine you've forgotten who's supposed to be in charge. How typically human. You are a forgetful bunch. I suppose it's utter chaos. No order. Frightening, really. I can see why you left."

"No, no. That's not it at all. We have leaders. We choose them ourselves. The people decide who they want to make the rules." Beth said, remembering her civics from school.

"Ghastly. Absolutely ghastly. I'd hate to see who ends up running your herd. Someone like that, probably." Ghandar pointed at his nephew, Vati, who was walking sideways like a crab, and then spinning around. Ryan was considering how a blow from the staff might alter the young elephant's behavior, but decided that it would probably shatter to splinters against the bull's iron skull. Beth laughed, and covered her mouth to keep the bugs from flying in. "He's really a very brave bull," Ghandar said. "But I think his sense slipped out of his trunk."

"How much further are we going, Ghandar?" Beth asked.

"There is an excellent place not far away." Ghandar mumbled.

"The grass bowl?" Drishad asked, breaking his silence.

"Yes, boy. You know this place?"

"There is good water. I hid for many days near there. I am sorry, Ghandar, for running, and my apologies to you as well, Beth. I meant no disrespect."

"How is it you can understand the elephants? I mean, I have this feather. How do you do it?"

"All of my family have this gift," He said softly. "In ancient times we were nobles in the city of Panagati. Lord Ganesh granted my family the knowledge of elephant speech after we freed him from a demon's trap. Each generation has this gift. In Rhamanapore, it is only the family of the Maharajah that still converse with the elephants."

"This is true," Gandhar muttered. "And even so, in Rhamanapore, your family allowed elephants to be taken as slaves and forced to do work and war."

"Yes," Drishad nodded. "What once was good is now evil. My grandfather was once wise, but he grew confused in his extreme age. He allowed Saudaheva to advise him, and agreed to many bad laws, but he still had some strength left. Saudaheva exceeded his authority, and sent armies to attack our neighbors. My grandfather was furious and had him exiled. Less than a week later, my grandfather, the Old Maharajah, collapsed after his dinner. He had seemed in good

80

health, before. In fact, he rode his mount around the grounds just that afternoon. But soon after his meal, he turned green and choked. He shouted that he was burning. He begged for us to put out the fire that burned him inside. He was like this for hours, and we could do nothing to help him. When breath left him, it was a mercy. Such a death was not natural. The kitchen staff said that they had seen a servant of Saudaheva's sneaking around the kitchen. Everyone felt that it was murder, but nothing could be proven. My uncle became the new Maharaja."

"We are here," Gandhar announced, as they came to the lip of a small cliff overlooking a large, bowl-like clearing. No trees grew within the hollow, but thick green grasses and ferns made a kind of meadow. Ledges of crumbling stone and gravel encircled the depression. The path crept down the face of a small cliff to the green pasture. Now they could see ragged clouds above. The final bits of color faded into the light gray of evening. At the bottom, Vati immediately began tearing up huge swaths of sweet grass, tucking bushels into his yawning mouth.

Ryan could hear water trickling somewhere behind his shoulder. It sounded like a spring in the rocks. Vati was only too happy to have him dismount. He followed the sound to a small pool, and drank his fill. Beth and Drishad joined him. The water was cold and sweet. They all felt better after they drank. There was a loud crashing from the meadow behind them. They ran back to find Gandhar and Vati pulling up trees, leaning them against each other for a shelter.

The gray had left the sky and now the jungle swelled with new sounds. The darkness was heavy and complete. Drishad pulled some stones from his tattered clothing and made sparks into a pile of dry weeds. Soon, he had a small fire. Ryan dug out a handful of berries he had brought from Laughing

81

Cloud's lodge. The children were starved. Drishad was used to not eating, but the cousins were miserable. Beth popped a dried berry in her mouth and chewed. At first it was tough and leathery, like a stale raisin. As she chewed it became squishy and spongy, with a flavor between a tomato and a strawberry. The berry seemed full of juice, and she ground on it like chewing gum. Ryan and Drishad also looked surprised as they ate the berry. The juice was sweet and sustaining, like a hearty soup. In a short time, they all felt full. Instead of swallowing the berry, Beth spat it out in her hand. It looked exactly as it had appeared when Ryan had handed it to her. She put it in her pocket.

Vati was still eating, tearing great hunks out of the meadow. Gandhar stood shock still, groaning slightly in his sleep. A circle of clear, starry sky spun above them. Even though it was still hot, the stars looked cold and bright, like sharp chips of ice. Lower on the horizon, she saw a bright star twirling and winking. Ryan noticed it too.

"Isn't that Modokana?"

"Yes, I think it is."

Their faces were warm in the dim firelight. They sat just in front of the shelter the elephants had propped together. Silently, they wondered if they would ever get home at all.

SAUDAHEVA'S TREACHERY

"What happened to your uncle, Drishad?" Beth asked. She had been kept wondering for long enough. Although Beth did not want to be rude, or upset Drishad any more than she had to, she knew she would not be able to sleep until he told her the rest of his story.

"He became the new Maharajah, and everything was fine for a while. Then, one day he received a gift from a neighboring king. It was supposedly a token of good will. A gesture of respect for the passing of the old Maharajah, and of hope for good relations with the new Maharajah."

"What was it?" Beth asked.

"Beautiful earrings, which are called karna, fashioned from enormous black pearls. My uncle always wore them. But they were enchanted. It was a trick from Saudaheva. While my uncle wore the karna, only Saudaheva's words would seem true. All other voices would be heard as lies. Soon, the Maharaja had that demon back in the palace as advisor, and it was worse than before. The more my family tried to tell my uncle of Saudaheva's lies, the more suspicious and angry he became. Enraged, he began to actually have his noble brothers and sisters executed and imprisoned, believing they were plotting against him." Drishad's voice had become a whisper, and he looked deeply into the fire. "He had my mother and father arrested and thrown into the dungeons deep beneath the palace. I never saw them again." The fire crackled and smoked. "I remember them very well. I remember when they were taken away. I did not understand then. I still do not understand."

"What did he say? What?" Ryan insisted. Beth had stopped translating, overcome with the sorrow she saw in Drishad's face. After a moment she relayed the rest of the story to Ryan.

"Well? How did he get away then? Why is he still alive?" Ryan demanded. Beth sighed and asked Drishad.

"My aunt, the queen, was very clever. She was the one who discovered the true nature of the karna. While my Uncle slept, she slipped off the earrings and handed them to a loyal guard. He smashed them into dust before Saudaheva's face. When my uncle awoke, he returned to his normal self. He was a kind and generous man, and with horror, he now saw the destruction he had caused his family and people. Immediately, he threw open the dungeon to free all those he had been so wrong to accuse. The sight of his dear friends and loved ones, broken and starving, was more than he could stand."

"He ransacked the castle searching for Saudaheva. But the sorcerer had not been idle. He had found secrets of the earth that let him control the very ground beneath his feet. Now, soldiers crafted from the clay of the mountain attacked my uncle and his bodyguard. They fought bravely, but how can you fight against soldiers made of dirt and gravel? Their weapons were blunted, and no sooner had they destroyed a company of clay men, then another party of soldiers arrived. Even so, they continued, until Saudaheva himself tired of the game. Finally taking the form of a great tiger, he fell upon the exhausted defenders, destroying and feasting on them."

"How did you escape?" Beth said.

"I did not escape, but I was spared."

"How?"

"By my aunt, the queen. Not only was she cunning, but she had the gift of prediction. There were times she could see events in the future. Everyone knew of her talent, and she was never wrong. Even Saudaheva feared and respected her. It was his intention to marry my aunt, justifying his place on the throne. She refused absolutely, even though Saudaheva swore it meant her own death. When that didn't work, he threatened to take my life unless she agreed. The queen just laughed. She told him that he had better protect me and keep me close, for she had foreseen that if he ever tried to take my life, he would

destroy himself. My aunt's reputation was such that Saudaheva was afraid, and spared me."

"And what happened to the queen?" Beth gasped.

"She was imprisoned. He lied to the people, saying she had agreed to marry him. Then he sent her to the dungeon. I never saw her again either. He kept me as a slave. I was forced to labor at Karhada. He began to transform our elegant palace into a keep, an evil fortress where he could rule over all the lands. There was a lot of work to do, trenches to dig, stones to carry, mortar to stir. I was fed just enough to live, and slept in a tower open to the sky."

"One day I was working on a wall, when there was an earthquake. A section of the cliff fell away, and my scaffolding slid on top. I tumbled along to the base of the hill. I awoke stunned, but by some miracle, not badly hurt. I ran into the jungle. The clay men pursued me, and even Saudaheva stalked the night, looking for my scent. I endured terror after terror to make it this far." His face grew dark in the shadows of the fire.

"Why did you come here? Why in the middle of the jungle? Aren't there other cities where you could get help?" Beth drew her knees up to her chest.

"At first I was just running anywhere, as long as it was away from Karhada, and then... Something else happened. One night Saudaheva was very close. I was hiding in a crevice when his men walked right by. I could feel the great cat, I knew he was close. I shut my eyes tight, and waited for the end. I have never been so afraid."

"To calm my shaking, I thought about my grandfather, who once told me stories about the ancient, far-away days, when we lived in the jungle with the elephants, and were a nation greater than any other. He would describe the ancient city of Panagati as if he had really lived there. He talked of the great Banyan tree, and all the magical things that came from it. They were beautiful stories. When I asked if they were true, he would whoop and laugh and tell me they were just stories. Then I would be sent off to bed."

"In that crevice, remembering those stories, I made a vow. If I lived, I would at least see this city with my own eyes, and find out if they were just stories. All the weeks I crawled through the jungle, I dreamed of someday rebuilding such a city. These dreams fed me when I had nothing to eat. When I was taken to Madriva, I couldn't believe my luck. But she has grown to fear and hate humans, and I was afraid to tell her my true name. I had come so close to Panagati. Now I will never see it." He shrugged his shoulders, and grinned nervously. His eyes were wet.

"Tell him he didn't miss much. A big pile of broken down rock," Ryan said.

"I'm not going to tell him that. He cares about it. It's his dream."

"I'm just trying to…" Ryan did not finish his sentence. A skittering of gravel tumbled on their right. Two seconds later they heard a crunching sound to their left.

"What's going on?" Beth jumped up, frightened. Now there were sounds all around them. There were things coming down into the hollow.

"It's them!" Drishad threw grass on the fire, and it flared high. "They've found me."

Battle in the Hollow

The bright fire exposed several shadowy forms approaching the shelter from all directions. Vati was awake and blew a tremendous blast as he rushed the closest figure. Gandhar was suddenly alert as well. He looked around carefully, assessing the situation. He moved toward the fire.

"Try not to move. Stay here, between us," he said, calm, but firm. He grabbed one of the smaller logs from the makeshift shelter with his trunk. "Do not get close. I need room." He swept the thick log menacingly, and charged a group of dark figures to the left.

The dark forms moved toward them stiffly, thicker and larger than ordinary men. They looked similar to the statues at Madriva's temple, crumbling copies of ancient gods and heroes. They were rougher, and more sinister, dripping clods as they approached slowly and deliberately.

"They are clay soldiers," Drishad murmured. "Men summoned from the mud."

The dirt men took no notice of the rampaging elephants, but marched steadily forward. Vati was gleefully stomping one after another. Gandhar was also making short work of the invaders, blasting two or three at a time into dust with each swipe of the log. In spite of their efforts, the clay men came on.

There were too many to count. The elephants were forced back as they began to tire, and the children were sprayed with flying dirt every time Gandhar made contact with his heavy club.

The children put their back to the fire, and Ryan gripped the staff like a baseball bat. The first rocky form stepped into the circle of light. Ryan jumped forward and rapped him in the middle with the staff. There was a flash as the figure disintegrated into a pile of earth and stones.

"That was easy!" He shouted. "I hardly even touched him." He ran to the next one and glanced him with the head of the staff. Dirt flew in an arc as he vanished. Ryan jumped over the fire, dispatching three more clay men. As Beth watched him, she heard a shout next to her. Drishad crumpled to the ground under a rocky fist. His head lolled as he was dragged away.

"Ryan! Over here!" Beth grabbed Drishad's foot, and was drug along behind him. She screamed as grating, stony hands snatched her waist. They were more like blunt claws, as powerful as pincers. She was lifted in the air, and for a moment stared full into the hideous misshapen face of the earth man that held her. His head was like a decrepit statue, a rough lump between his shoulders, with weathered holes for eyes and mouth. He smelled like sour mud. She saw him only for a moment before he disintegrated into a pile of muck, dropping her. Ryan danced by, slicing and prodding with the staff.

"Sorry, Beth!" he shouted. "They're all over the place!"

There were mounds of dirt everywhere now, and Drishad sat up in one, shaking his head clear. Beth ran to him and helped him up. They had to jump away quickly as Vati backed into them, almost squashing the kids beneath his feet. He

smacked one soldier with his trunk, knocking him into another hard enough so they both flew apart. He kicked backwards and smacked the torso out of a clay giant just reaching for Drishad. Beth held Drishad up, staying close to Ryan and trying to avoid the gyrations of the two elephants. Gandhar had thrown away the log, and was tossing the clay figures over his back where they smashed into pieces in the meadow.

With the staff, Ryan was destroying most of the dirt army. One touch was all he needed, and they fell apart into clods. They were all weary when suddenly there were no more of the enemy. The meadow was now filled with piles of earth, but nothing moved. The elephants swayed from exhaustion, even Vati stood still, blowing hard from his exertions.

"If the Demon is with them, he will come now," Drishad mumbled, pulling branches off the shelter and stoking the fire. He had recovered from the blow, but blood trickled down his forehead and he was very pale. Ryan turned and ran up a dirt mound to have a look. There was nothing but darkness. A cracking, rushing sound came from the direction of the pool they had drunk from earlier.

"What is it?" Beth asked, outlined by the light from the fire.

"I can't tell." Ryan searched the darkness, gripping the staff. "I need some light. I can't see."

The staff began to glow with a warm yellow light, like sunshine. Ryan held it up in amazement, and looked back in the direction of the sound. There, he saw water boiling and spewing from the ground. It cascaded from the side of the hollow, splashing into the meadow. As he watched , a dirty brown stream snaked between the mounds toward them. He gestured to the others.

"Come up, climb the mounds! They're flooding the hollow!" As he shouted, the filthy pool rushed into the circle around the shelter, melting the smaller mounds into mud. Rushing water splashed over Beth and Drishad's feet. The fire went out with a great hiss of steam. Ryan held the staff up so they could see, and they climbed up next to him. The water was rising fast. The elephants were already wading knee-deep towards the humans.

"Get on my back," Gandhar commanded, "And we will carry you out."

The children did as he asked, getting soaked in the process. They moved towards the edge of the meadow, but the pool was rising quickly. Beth's teeth were chattering from the cold water. She and Drishad were dunked as Gandhar slipped. He was swimming more than wading now, and the water came to his shoulder. He held his trunk high up, like a snorkel, to breathe.

Beth and Drishad clung tightly to Ghandar's loose skin as the water began to rush over his back. Ahead they heard Vati splashing with Ryan waving the staff, making crazy shadows on the water. By the yellow light, they saw the small cliff that bordered the hollow. Vati came to the edge and began to climb out. The bank was steep, and he searched for a good foothold. Gandhar reached the edge and did the same. The cliff was loose and crumbling. The elephants were wet, and it made the ground slippery. With a great effort, Vati pulled himself out of the water and discovered a ledge that led up to the top. It was just wide enough for him to creep along. Gandhar was tired, and carried more weight, and it took him a little longer to get out of the water.

Vati moved along the ledge. He was close to the top now. Beth heard a cracking, crumbling sound, and then Ryan shouted. They were pelted by loose rocks as the ledge gave way under Vati. The great animal rolled down the steep bank and Ryan was thrown clear. The staff flew from his hands and the light went out. He tumbled along with Vati into Gandhar and everyone was knocked back into the dark, cold, water with a tremendous splash.

Beth spluttered to the surface. She heard water splashing all around her. She shouted for Ryan and Drishad, but there was no answer. She heard mighty gurgling sounds and blowing, like one of the elephants, but they did not answer either. Her hand smacked a rock, and she realized she was next to the bank. She climbed up, and shouted again for Ryan. She could see nothing, and felt only wet rocks and water. Something brushed her cheek. It was the feather, slipping from her bedraggled hair. She stuffed it into her pocket along with the acorn. She had nearly swallowed it when she fell.

"Beth!" she heard, "I'm looking for you! Where are you?"

"I'm here!" she shouted. It was Ryan's voice, but it came from above her. She wondered how he managed to get out already. "Where's Drishad?" she called, but there was no answer. She heard splashing still, but farther off to her left. On her right, there was the softer sound of dripping water, and a low moaning. She moved carefully over the rocks, climbing higher. The water was still rising. The moaning grew louder. She heard rocks skittering behind her. She turned quickly and slipped into a hammer of darkness.

KARHADA KEEP

When Beth awoke, she wished she hadn't. Her eyes were covered and she was strapped to some kind of stretcher or bier. Her head throbbed, and felt like a split pumpkin. A spot just above her forehead itched terribly. Apart from turning her head and moving her hand slightly, she could not move. She pitched and jolted as she lay, and realized she was being carried, and not very gently. She could smell the sour muck of the clay people all around. Her mouth was gagged, and she could only make a muffled groan. When she did, other moans answered, somewhere in front and behind her. It was some comfort to know she was not alone.

They marched on and on, with almost no rest. Occasionally, they were allowed to eat and drink, still blindfolded. The clay people stuffed handfuls of some kind of grain into their mouths. It tasted like mold and dirt from their paws. The dirt soldiers never stopped to sleep, but pressed on through the night.

A sharp barb on one of the branches that made up her bier poked her in the side. She scooted away as best as she could. Using the sharp edge of the branch, she rubbed the rough vine her hands were tied together with. It took a long time, but she managed to free one hand. Very slowly she slipped it into her pocket and found the berry. She popped it in her mouth and lay completely still. The berry juice filled her belly and she felt stronger.

The going was smoother now and she imagined they were on some kind of road. She managed to loosen the blindfold, and she saw two biers like hers, with Ryan and Drishad trussed up on each. They were held on the shoulders of marching earth men. She assumed this was the common road Madriva had mentioned. Remembering Madriva made her think of the brave elephants. She wondered what had become of them.

Beth tried to keep her mind off the steady tromping of the soldiers. She thought about sitting comfortably at home, reading a book, but it was useless. Thinking of anything pleasant soon became impossible. The jarring gait of her bearers rattled her with every step. At first, Beth and Ryan just felt sorry for themselves, wondering what they had done to deserve such poor treatment. Then they worried about each other. After a while, they started thinking of all the good things they had at home that they missed, that they took for granted. They each made silent promises to be better people, to live differently, if they could only escape. But the march continued, until they had almost no hope of ever seeing their home again.

But as bad as Beth and Ryan felt, it was worse for Drishad. The cousins had no idea where they were going or what would happen to them, but Drishad did. As tough as things had been for him alone in the jungle, his life had been a daydream compared with the nightmare that came closer with each step. Every moment was an agony as he remembered with horror what he had escaped, and what lay before them.

The earth men marched on the road for a long time, before turning and heading up into the mountains. They climbed higher and higher, and it became very cold. Beth had laid so long in the same way that she felt bruised all over, and each bump was painful. Soon they began to descend again, winding down along the side of a great hill. Peeking under the gap in her blindfold she saw they were going down into an enormous valley. The broad streak of a river wound around the base of a smaller mountain, ringed by a rocky range. This hill seemed to command the entire valley. On the top, barely visible, she could make out blunt towers squatting on heavy battlements.

As she suspected, once they reached the valley floor, they started climbing again up the smaller mountain. The pain had grown intolerable, and she paid little attention to what happened around her until she was finally dumped with the others onto cold stone. They were untied and their blindfolds and gags removed. It was some time before they recovered enough to sit up and look around, squinting from the light. They were too dazed and stunned to even speak.

They were in the courtyard of the old palace. There had once been trees, but they were now stripped bare. Machinery and strange weapons were pushed against the walls. Earth men stood everywhere, staring blankly. Some sunlight filtered through high gray clouds, and wind shrieked, gusting over the high turrets. The palace had been altered. The windows were bricked up into arrow slits, and the doors were gated and barred. All worked stone and finery was stripped or stained black from the oily smoke drifting out of grates in the foundation. It was a dismal and forbidding place.

Beth was the first to stand. The berry juice had sustained her, and she still had some strength. Her legs and feet did not want to work, but she forced them. Her whole body was sore and aching. Ryan was sitting up, shaking his head clear, but Drishad just lay in a heap, unmoving.

"Are you all right, Ryan?" She staggered over to him, and tried to help him stand. "Do you still have that berry?" He

nodded his head, pulling it from his pocket. He chewed for a moment while she went to Drishad. He was curled up in a ball, his hands covering his head. His eyes were squeezed shut, and he did not respond to Beth's prodding. She saw he was breathing, and left him alone. Ryan stood slowly. He was very pale. He reached his hand out to Beth, too dizzy to stand on his own. They slowly moved in a circle, and the stiffness gradually wore off.

"I lost the staff, Beth," Ryan muttered. "I'm sorry. I'm sure that's what we needed to get back. I don't know how we'll get home now."

"It's all right, Ryan. We'll get back just fine. We'll find someone that can contact the police or something, and they'll come get us. We're not involved in this fight. They've got to let us go." Beth smiled, but Ryan just shook his head.

"They can't. I've been thinking about it. Look at this place. It's not where we are. It's when we are. They don't have phones because they don't exist. We're stuck. If magic brought us here, it'll have to take us back. That's why we needed that staff. I don't know how we'll manage to get back now." Beth's heart sank, as she realized what he said made sense. Ryan had knocked down her last hope, until a new idea occurred to her.

"Maybe this Saudaheva isn't as bad as they say. He knows magic. Maybe we can get him to send us back. Let's ask Drishad if there's something we can offer him. Here, help me out. He's like a bag of rocks." Together, they managed to get Drishad up and moving, but he would not speak or look in their eyes.

"Come on, Drishad. What's wrong with you? Here." Ryan stuck a dried berry in his mouth, and the boy started to chew.

"Why won't you speak to us, Drishad? What's happened to you?" Beth said softly, leaning over to look at his face.

"We are all lost. It is my fault. You fought bravely and look what it has done," Drishad croaked, not raising his head.

"It's not your fault. Maybe we can do something to make a deal with Saudaheva." Beth rubbed Drishad's cold hands between hers.

"There are no deals with him. He takes what he wants, and if you are left with your life, you are lucky indeed. If you have something of value, he will find it and strip it away. If you don't want to be hurt, then give it up quickly and without a fight. He is not a man, Beth. He is a demon."

"Now, now, young man! That is no way to talk of your trusting guardian." A powerful voice bellowed behind the children. Drishad shouted and fell to the ground, covering his head. Beth and Ryan spun quickly to see a magnificent figure, a giant of a man dressed in elaborate silks and jewels, with a great oiled beard and mustache. His head was crowned with an elaborate turban of silk, fashioned with the stars of the night sky.

"Some guests are never satisfied, I fear. I hope you two will not be as unappreciative as this gutter rat."

"Beth, I can understand him! He can speak English," Ryan exclaimed.

"Yes. I can speak in all tongues. You will find that I am full of surprises. Come."

The sorcerer turned and walked toward the gate of the palace. Beth and Ryan limped behind. Drishad lay in a heap on the ground.

Beneath the Palace

"What about Drishad?" Beth whispered. Saudaheva turned on his heel and glared at them.

"He has a special chamber, you know. He has been a bad boy and will be sent to his room to ponder his behavior. I will deal with him later. Now, don't try my patience. Follow me." With a gesture from the magician, the heavy bolts and enormous gates flew open as if they were made of cardboard. The children hurried to follow the man dressed in orange and black silk as he stalked through the dark archway of the keep.

The interior of the palace was not much better. It was like a cavern, with wrought iron torch holders and caches of weapons arranged against the walls. The roof arched high overhead, the ribs pocked and crumbling. The floor was once a mosaic, now cracked and smashed. In some places the figures of gods and animals could still be seen, dancing through the steps of some elaborate story. Beth and Ryan did not have much time to look before they had popped down a narrow staircase behind Saudaheva.

Beth and Ryan both felt foolish, following a man they had heard so many terrible things about. At this point, they had no other choice. They both felt that Saudaheva was not the kind of person that you questioned or complained to.

The staircase was very steep and had no landings. It spiraled down, deep below the palace. The air was very stale and musty. Ryan had to steady himself against the wall as he went down. The stone was damp and slimy, with large patches of pale mold.

"You know, I don't often entertain guests in my home," Saudaheva said over his shoulder. "I think it's nice to meet someone who is not from around here. I imagine you've had quite the adventure."

"Yes we have," Ryan muttered.

"I myself travel quite a bit. I find the change of scenery to be good for the spirit. But let me confess this: no matter how much I enjoy the trip, it's always a relief to get back home. Wouldn't you agree?" He had come to the bottom of the staircase. There was a large wooden door with enormous hinges.

"Here we are." He clapped his hands together and the door flew open, clanging against the rock. They entered a strange room, lit by a queer blue light from a high ceiling. Heavy tables were everywhere, covered with strange liquids bubbling in flasks, ancient books, bizarre instruments, and many gruesome items which the children could not and did not want to recognize. The smell was horrifying.

"Yes, I'm afraid the ventilation is rather poor," Saudaheva muttered, "But the privacy is absolute, and I find that this is the only place I can really concentrate. Now that this palace is mine alone, I still prefer to work down here. Isn't that odd?" He had an unpleasant way of showing all of his teeth when he grinned. His strong, white teeth looked sharp against the midnight black of his shiny beard and mustache. It was startling, and put the hair up on Beth's neck.

"But enough about me. Let's talk about you two. My, but you've had a long journey. I've noted with interest the powers

the two of you have displayed. Perhaps you can tell me where you came about them. Let's start with the cave at Panagati." The sorcerer sat down and rubbed his long beard.

"Uh… There's really not much to tell. We were in this cave, and… You know, we were lost, and couldn't find our way out, and… We just kind of came out in the salt cave." Ryan was unsure of what to say. The magician seemed pleasant, but Ryan didn't understand enough of what had

102

happened to them to explain any of it. He also had a feeling that he should not trust this man.

"Very interesting, but not very detailed. Why don't you tell me how you came to be lost in the cave to begin with."

"Well, there was this tree, this really big tree, a long time ago," Ryan noticed that Saudaheva perked up at the mention of the tree. "And I guess it left these caves in the ground from it's roots, and we were just, you know, looking around. And we got lost. That's it."

"Hmmm. I still get the feeling that you are not being completely honest with me." As he spoke, Saudaheva fingered an enormous amber diamond that swung from a gold chain around his neck. "I know of this tree. Indeed, I thought I was alone in my understanding of the great tree's lore. You see, I'm a kind of collector. I've been able to learn many secrets and discover a few trinkets by exploring those caves, just as you have. What interests me in particular is that staff of yours. How did you acquire it?"

"Oh… I just found it… In the cave."

"It was just lying there, on the ground, in the cave." Saudaheva raised an eyebrow.

"That's right."

"And you just happened to know how to perform all these tricks with it, blowing down doors, making light, vanquishing my poor troops. Just like that?"

"Exactly. How did you find out about…?"

"I know a great deal about you, Ryan, and you too, Beth." He smiled unpleasantly again. Ryan was gripped with fear, wondering how the sorcerer had discovered their names. The magicians waggled a finger at Ryan. "It seems clear to me that you are a magician of some small talent. Perhaps, you may be of service to me. First, I need to know all you know.

103

Everything." Saudaheva's eyes burned in a way that made the boy's stomach tremble. Right then, Ryan knew that this man was never going to help him. He realized with absolute clarity that once the demon was finished extracting information from them, they would be disposed of. He shut his mouth tight, staring defiantly at the wall.

"Well. I suppose I'll have to discuss this with your cousin." He turned to Beth. "Now, little girl, I suppose you've had enough of this journey, yes?" She nodded sadly and looked away. "I imagine that you are probably ready to go home. I can make that happen, you know."

"You can?" Beth asked hopefully.

"Of course. I have the power to send you back with the snap of my fingers."

Ryan saw that Beth believed Saudaheva, and he opened his mouth to tell her the magician was lying. No words came out. Saudaheva saw him out of the corner of his eye and smirked. Ryan tried to speak again, but he could not. The words seemed stuck in his throat.

"Well, Ryan, you didn't want to talk, and now it seems you can't. What's the matter, cat got your tongue?" Saudaheva's laughter trailed into what sounded like the snarl of a panther. "Now, Beth. Before I send you back, maybe you can tell me where you learned these powers of yours, and who, if anyone, helped you. Oh, and don't forget to mention where you found that staff."

"How do I know you'll send me back after I tell you all that stuff?"

"Oh very well, I give you my word. That should make you happy. Now please continue, my dear."

"I don't trust you."

"Of course not. Why should you? But if you don't tell me, then I'll have to be more persuasive, and I don't think you want that." As Beth watched, Saudaheva's eyes grew larger and his face began to swell. Orange streaks ran through his beard, and his grin became menacing as the teeth twisted into razor sharp points. Beth's heart stopped and she froze in fear as he leaned toward her. The tiger's red tongue flicked out, scraping the end of her nose. The tiger's head growled ferociously and his breath was like rotten meat. Beth could not breathe. There was a thumping on the door behind Saudaheva, and quick as a flash, he returned to his human form. An earthen soldier stood in the doorway. Saudaheva jumped up suddenly.

"What is it? Can't you see I'm busy?" The dirt figure mumbled something, it sounded like gravel in a coffee can.

"What? That's not possible. The fools. Well, they will soon be very sorry for this mistake. Very sorry, indeed." He turned back to Beth, pale and frozen in place.

"Well, children, I've enjoyed our little game, but I have no more time to play. Here! You! Strap them to that table!" The clay trooper grabbed the children, securing them side by side to the only empty table in the room. Saudaheva glided over to them, glowering at the children.

"You will find I am not the only resident that enjoys having guests. Soon, you will be quite eager to tell me what I wish to know, and end your suffering." Saudaheva chuckled, ending again in the tiger's purr. He sidled to the door, and the light blinked out as he snapped his fingers. The room was plunged into thick, heavy darkness.

"Sweet dreams, children. Nighty-night." The door boomed shut. Beth and Ryan were left alone in the midnight blackness of Saudaheva's dungeon.

19

RATS

"It just keeps getting better and better," Ryan said, shaking in terror. "Are you all right, Beth? I'm glad that dirt boy came down when he did. I thought Saudaheva was going to gobble you up like little red riding hood."

"Yeah. I'm O.K., I guess." Her heart was still pounding in her chest like a timpani, but she could breathe again. Those ferocious eyes had paralyzed her.

"Did you hear what that mud man said when he came down the stairs?"

"No, it just sounded like mumbling to me. What did he say?"

"Just one word. Elephants. What do you think about that?"

"That could mean anything. Maybe he has allies that just arrived. Maybe they found some elephants that he's been looking for. Maybe he's having elephant for dinner. Who knows? I'm more interested in what he was talking about when he said he wasn't the only resident happy to see us. What is that supposed to mean?"

"I don't know. Maybe we're not alone in here."

"That's a nice thought." Ryan pulled on the ropes he was secured with, but they were too tight. He could feel Beth shaking with fear against him.

106

"What's that sound?" Beth hissed. Ryan listened, but there was only silence.

"I don't hear anything. It's your imagination. Nothing else is down here. Who else could stand the smell?"

"I'm telling you there is something else in here," Beth muttered. In the silence, there was a distinct skittering sound and some kind of squeak.

"O.K., I heard it that time. Maybe it's just a mouse or something." With shock Ryan realized that even if it was only a rodent, he was tied up and completely helpless. He pulled the ropes on his wrist with a new vigor. He had not been able to eat much in the last few days, and the skin was loose on his wrist. After wriggling carefully, he slowly began to work one hand out of the knots. Just then, he could hear some kind of

scratching noises on the leg of the table they were tied to. He pulled against the ropes harder. Beth screamed in the darkness, and wiggled violently on the table.

"Something is on me! Something is on my leg!" Ryan pulled his hand free, but the rest of his body was still tied down. He flailed his arm over Beth, brushing off something furry and heavy. It fell off the table and squealed. Now they could hear many more sounds of scratching and skittering all around them.

"Where's the acorn? Beth! Where's the acorn?"

"It's in my pocket, on the left, but I can't reach it."

"I think I can. Hold on." Ryan dug in Beth's pocket and pulled the acorn out. Stretching his hand up, he bent his head as far down as he could against the ropes and was just able to pop it in his mouth.

"All right, you critters!" He shouted in the most aggressive voice he could muster with an acorn in his mouth. "Quit trying to climb up here. I've got nothing against you, but I'll kill the first one that tries to get up here again."

"They say they don't care. They're hungry. They don't get much to eat down here." Beth, of course, still had the feather and she could hear what the rats were saying.

"The master of this castle will be very upset if you eat us. He has plans and needs information from us to fulfill them," Ryan shouted.

"They're laughing, Ryan. They say if we're so important, then why are we tied up in the dark?"

"Good point. I guess that does look pretty bad for us."

"They also say that Saudaheva is not the master of this castle. They are. They say that they know all the secrets of this fortress, all the hiding spots. They are the true masters of Karhada Keep."

"I don't believe you!" Ryan said to the rats. "If you are the true masters of this castle, then why do you hang around down here, hungry and whining? I tell you what, if you really are the ones that run this palace, then tell me where Drishad's chamber is."

Ryan was silent for a moment as Beth listened intently to the squeaking in the darkness.

"They say that Drishad is in an open room in one of the towers, facing the North wind. It's so cold and barren in that part of the palace that they rarely go there, but they check on him every month or so hoping that he's dead."

"That's gross."

"They said they were hungry."

"I think I'd rather have no visitors at all. You think he's still in that tower now?"

"Wait a minute… They say they'd eat out of the pantries in the kitchen, but the servants keep the larder locked, and they can't get in."

"Look, rats! If you help us get free, then we'll all head for the kitchens and I will personally pass out the rat chow, O.K.?"

"They agree. Don't forget about Drishad."

"I know. Oh… Yuck…" The rats had scurried up onto the kids and were chewing on the ropes that bound them. Even though Beth and Ryan knew that the rats had agreed to help, it was not a very pleasant feeling to be lying tied up in the dark with rodents clambering all over them.

After they were freed, the children stumbled around in the dark looking for the exit, but Beth followed the rats' voices as they led them to the door.

"I'm not sure if their doing this because they're really hungry or because of their pride," Beth said in the dark. "It seems like they really want to show us that this is their castle. You wouldn't think that rats thought so much of themselves. Is the door locked?"

"No. I guess he didn't think it was very likely that we would get up off that table."

Ryan pushed the door open and felt his way up the first step. The rats squeezed in around their feet and hopped up the stairs with them. This was also an unpleasant sensation, but they were starting to get used to it. Beth's spirits lifted a little higher with every step they took away from the dungeon. When they got to the top, light streamed in. Beth tugged on Ryan's shirt as he reached the first stair.

"They say they're going through the walls to get to the kitchen. If we go right down to the second big archway, walk all the way down and turn left where it ends, that's the main kitchen."

"If this is their castle, why do they have to hide?" Ryan snickered.

"They say it's a lot quicker to go their way." Beth said, smiling.

Ryan looked to the left and quickly darted out into the hallway, smacking into a dirt guard. It was hard enough to knock Ryan to the ground. The soldier took no notice of him, and continued walking on some errand. Beth trundled up behind Ryan and helped him up.

"That hurt. It's like running into a wall," He said, brushing off bits of dirt.

"You're lucky. They must be too stupid to be surprised."

"Well, I guess that means I must be smart. Let's hurry."

They ran down the hallway. As they turned into the second archway they were surprised again by a small group of dirt men. The soldiers again took no notice of them and continued marching down the main hallway.

"Don't they see us?" Beth gasped, breathless.

"Maybe they're like robots. They only do what they're programmed to do."

The kids made it to the kitchens and scurried back to the pantries, an entire wall of cabinets and cupboards. For the first time, they got a good look at their rodent friends, and it took their breath away. There were dozens of them, some as large as small cats, with matted gray and black fur, enormous yellow teeth, and long, pallid tails.

"They're huge! I've never seen rats that big," Ryan gasped.

"Yeah, and they're hungry too, That big gray one says to hurry up. They've been waiting. He's the one we've been talking to" The huge rat tilted back on his hind feet, bristling his whiskers at Ryan.

"O.K. buddy, you'll get your food, but you have to agree to show me where Drishad is." The rat cocked his head and fixed a beady eye on Ryan.

"He agrees, but he doesn't seem too happy about it. He won't show you, but he'll tell you how to get there. He says it wasn't part of the deal."

The doors to the pantries had clever handles, latching securely with curved pins. Ryan popped out the pins and threw open the doors. The rats swarmed in and began feasting. Ryan was starving too, and he grabbed loaves of bread. He handed one to Beth and started tearing into his. He rummaged around and came up with some fruit that looked like red oranges. The juice was sweet as he bit into them. Beth stuffed her pockets with nuts and dried fruits that she found in one of the bins. The big rat directed them to Drishad's room and they bolted out of the kitchens.

They ran out into the main hallway and up an enormous staircase. Clay troops were all around, but they took no notice, and the children lost their caution with them. Almost all the troops were armed with weapons, long cruel halberds with shining blades. They were all shuffling to the main gate in their slow, pondering gait. Just then, the children felt, rather than heard, a heavy thump that seemed to shake the castle. As they continued up the stairs, they felt it again.

"Something is going on, Ryan," Beth panted as they ran up the steps.

"I know. Those dirt boys looked like they were heading for some action."

They reached the top of the steps and shot down a smaller hallway that led out to the wall. They passed through a guardhouse, and were on the battlements.

"Wait, Beth, let me catch my breath," Ryan wheezed, leaning on the outside wall.

They were high up on the side of the keep now, at the base of the towers. Far below, she could make out dust rising in front of the main gates. She saw brown figures and large gray humps moving together.

"Elephants!" she shouted to Ryan. "Look, look!" She hopped up and down on the wall.

Ryan peered over the wall and watched the battle. The sun was beginning to set, and the dust rising from the gates was pink and orange. Suddenly he saw another streak of orange, with a flash of white and black. There, standing in the courtyard was the tiny form of Saudaheva, and he was turned towards them, motionless.

"Watch out! Get down!" Ryan hissed, but he knew it was too late. He could feel the magician's gaze on them as he crouched.

"What is it?" Beth whispered.

"It's Saudaheva. He saw me, I think. We've got to hurry."

THE NORTH TOWER

Beth and Ryan hurried along the walkway on the top of the wall. Ryan caught one more glimpse of the courtyard. Brown figures were lining up and marching back to the main hall.

"Bad news, Beth. I think the dirt boys were just sent to fetch us."

"We're almost there. As slow as they move, it'll take some time for them to get up here. We can grab Drishad, and get out of here."

"How? I don't know my way around this place. Do you know a way out?"

"We'll figure it out later. Here, up this staircase."

The children reached another guardhouse at the base of a high tower. They flew up a flight of steps and came to a thick door. It was bolted on the outside. They threw back the lock and pulled it open. They walked into a partially destroyed room. Half the roof and part of the wall had crumbled away. They could see the valley stretching away into the Northern range. Drishad was huddled in a filthy blanket in the far corner.

"Come on, Drishad! Get up!" Ryan rocked his shoulder. Drishad looked up, blinking his eyes.

"Hurry! We don't have much time," Beth entreated.

"It's a trick," he mumbled, laying back down. "He's just playing a game with you. He'll grab you in a moment and it will be worse than before."

"Get up! We've got to try. You've got to get away. Do it for your family. You're the only one left. Come on. We need to go!"

"What's the point?"

"The elephants are storming the gates. They're fighting Saudaheva. Maybe we can hook up with them."

"Really? I thought I heard something before, but…"

"We've got a chance. Let's go. Now!"

Together, Ryan and Beth pulled Drishad up, with the blanket still around him. They dashed out of the room and down to the guardhouse. Along the wall, the clay soldiers were marching toward them.

"Quick! This way!" Beth looked around and saw the great gray rat hugging the corner near another arched hall.

"Ryan, it's the rat! He says to go this way."

The three children rushed to follow the rat through the doorway and to another steep stairway. They climbed flight after flight of stone steps.

"This isn't right," Drishad said. "We're going up the north tower. We can't get out this way!"

"The rat says there's a secret way from the top," Beth huffed as they ran up the stairs. "Only the rats know about it." Behind them she heard the scraping of gravelly feet on the stone. The clay men were not far behind.

They finally burst out at the top of the tower. It was a round, empty room, with great arched windows in the stone. A doorway led to a wide balcony around the tower.

"Where's the way out?" Ryan gasped.

"Just step off and you'll be out of this keep," the rat chuckled, "Or if you'd rather not, just stay put and the troops will escort you downstairs. Either way, I'm assured of another meal."

Beth tried to kick the rat, but he danced out of the way, slipping down the stairs.

They tricked us, Ryan," Beth moaned. "There's no way out. We're trapped." The last sunlight vanished behind the hill and the faint pink in the sky turned ashen. It was shadowy in the tower and difficult to see. Drishad laughed nervously.

"You see? He always wins. No matter what."

"Why don't you shut your mouth. At least we tried," Ryan snapped. "I thought you were pretty brave, but you've been nothing but a sniveling little goof ever since they dumped us here. We shouldn't have tried to save you. We could've been out of this place if we hadn't come up here."

"You wouldn't understand. If you knew what he had done to…"

"Save it, Drishad. You were right. Tiger-man got us. Happy?"

"What are we going to do now?" Beth asked, her face dim in the evening.

"Let me think for a minute." Ryan walked towards the balcony.

"Hey, I don't hear them anymore." Beth poked her head down the stairwell, "I think they've stopped on the steps."

"Of course. We are trapped, the elephants have gone, and now Saudaheva comes himself to devour you. But not me. He will keep me here to torture."

"Why don't you try to help, instead of creeping us out?" Ryan said, flashing a disgusted expression at Drishad.

Ryan stepped through the doorway and ran into the most hideous face he had ever seen. Leathery and brown, with huge bulbous eyes and a pig nose, it hung upside down and stared at him through slit eyelids. Ryan shouted and the creature opened a red mouth lined with rows of razor teeth. Huge leathery membranes flapped the air as the creature screeched and screamed.

"Ahhh! Help! What is this…" Ryan fell to the floor, covering his head. Beth was surprised too, but she had not run smack into the creature, and she recovered quickly.

"Calm down Ryan! You just surprised him. It's a bat." Beth ran to help Ryan up.

"That's the biggest bat I've ever seen."

"Hush! He's trying to say something… He says you scared him, but he forgives you 'cause it's almost time to wake up anyway." She could see a whole row of huge bats clinging to the eaves of the tower room.

"Sorry," Ryan muttered. "Do you know a way off this tower?"

"Not without wings, he says. Which, of course, is not a problem for them," Beth translated.

Ryan found it strange to have a conversation with a creature hanging upside down. "We're running from Saudaheva, will you help us get off this tower?"

Beth nodded her head as she listened to the bat. "They don't like the magician. They say the old Maharajah would feed them from his hand."

"I remember that. I do." Drishad said softly. "I used to catch giant moths and other insects, and my grandfather and I would toss them off this balcony for the bats to catch." He smiled, "They are amazing fliers, truly." He picked himself up from where he had slumped against the wall.

117

"They say Saudaheva captures them and uses their wings in his potions. They hate him. They want the old Maharajah back." Beth translated.

"Tell them I am the young Maharajah," Drishad said, standing erect and putting an imperious look on his face. In the dim light on the balcony, Beth was surprised. He really did look like a prince, in spite of his rags and injuries. "Tell them it is my pleasure that they should take us off this tower." Ryan relayed the exact message to the bat.

"They agree, although they seem nervous about it," Beth said. "He says that we're too heavy, and they could only glide us down to the forest. He says they might be able to do it, but it'll take three per person. I count six here now. That means they'll have to make two trips."

"If it works," Ryan muttered, and the bat nodded its head and blinked.

"It will work," Drishad stated. "You two go first. I will try to give you some time."

Beth and Ryan stood on the edge of the balcony. They were on the tallest tower of a castle on a high hill. Beth peered over into the blackness. Fortunately for her, the darkness concealed how far the drop was. Climbing on top of that balcony's ledge was the hardest thing the children had ever done. They stood there, swaying in the wind, and Beth clutched Ryan's hand and closed her eyes. He squeezed her hand as well, and then sidestepped away to make room between them. The bats launched from the eaves, swept around the tower, and came around for the children.

They were snatched off the wall with a jolt that knocked the breath out of Beth's lungs, and she fell into the darkness with the bats' wings beating all around her. A third pair of claws grabbed the legs of her jeans, and she felt her descent slowing. She dared to open her eyes, and saw they were gliding past the rocks of the hills, skimming over the trees. She made out the fluttering of other wings below and to her right, and saw Ryan outlined in moonlight. She looked below her shoulder, under her arm and saw the dark form of Karhada palace grow smaller. She smiled as the wind raked back her hair.

21

DRISHAD'S STAND

Drishad peered over the ledge, but it was no use. It was too dark, and he could not see his friends. He climbed on top of the ledge. Drishad had worked on the walls of the fortress for much of his life, and had no fear of heights. Exposed to the wind, he listened carefully, but heard nothing.

"I hope you're not thinking of doing anything drastic. Although you would be doing me a favor by extinguishing your pathetic life." Drishad did not need to turn around to recognize the voice. Fear stabbed him in the belly.

"Although I must admit, I would miss the entertainment of watching you suffer," Saudaheva continued, his voice a soft purr. "And I have some new ideas that will make your previous labors seem like idleness."

"Gloat while you can, Demon!" Drishad turned, wearing his princely expression, and locking his legs so his knees would not quake. "You will soon pay for all your misdeeds."

Shock was plain on the sorcerers face. Drishad noted with surprise the impression his manner made on the sorcerer. It was a momentary slip, and Saudaheva quickly grew a savage smile to cover it.

"Silence, boy! Or I will do worse than you can possibly imagine."

"Haven't you wondered where the rest of your prey has gone?" Drishad drew strength from the effect his confidence was having on the magician.

"I already know, rat! They lie broken on the rocks at my feet. They were smart to jump. Smarter than others here."

"Is your spectral vision as muddy as that? They are not dead. On the contrary. They came to this tower to cast their incantations and return to the world of spirits. They have power you cannot imagine. They are even now raising a ghostly army to cast you down and return me to my family's throne."

"Why do they leave you then, eh?" Saudaheva growled, rubbing the amber diamond around his neck.

"They have no fear of you. You can do nothing to stop them, and your own weakness keeps you from destroying me. I am protected by your fear, Demon. Your fear of my old Auntie. Ha!" Drishad snapped his fingers at the sorcerer. Saudaheva's face darkened, and his left eye twitched. "Tell me how it is that such a powerful sorcerer is paralyzed by a fortune-teller? You have left me alive so that I can watch your humiliation and defeat. Rhamanapore will be restored to my family, and I will toast the health of your enemies with a cup made from your skull." Drishad felt fire in his veins as he taunted the magician. It was wonderful to drive him insane with anger. But he knew it would not be long before the evil man snapped, and Drishad listened intently for the return of flapping wings.

"You insolent... foolish... How dare you... impudent..." Saudaheva's face was contorted with rage, his mouth spluttered and foamed. "I will tear you into rags... I will rip you..." As Drishad watched, the demon fell to the ground, twisting and growing as the bright gold stripes wrapped around him. His words faded into a roaring snarl as he raised

121

the head of a ferocious tiger, teeth bared. Infuriated, he swiped a paw full of white daggers at Drishad. The boy danced away on the wall, just avoiding the terrible claw. For a moment, the enormous tiger glared at him, his eyes shining red in the darkness. The beast erupted in an ear-splitting roar, echoing off the mountains. Beth and Ryan heard it far away, and were sad as they realized Drishad had met his end. The great cat settled on its haunches, ready to devour the boy.

Drishad knew there was no time left. The cat's lips were pulled back and the eyes grew large. The muscles in its legs tightened. Like a coiled spring or striking cobra, the tiger pounced. The slick teeth, like small swords, reached for Drishad. Suddenly, the boy hopped backwards off the balcony and into the dark air, and the teeth clashed on nothing at all. Now the huge animal realized the peril of falling, and tried to draw the leap short. The tiger's claws grasped and clawed the cold air. The beast hurtled over the tower's ledge, flailing at the darkness.

As he hung precariously, Drishad's chest burned from scraping the wall, but the agony from his hands and arms eclipsed everything. His fingers gripped the stone ledge of the balcony as he swung his feet, trying to pull himself up. He was too weak. His toes dangled into nothingness and slipped on the smooth walls of the tower. As his legs swung and kicked, his left hand suddenly popped off the ledge, and he felt the fingers of his right hand slipping. He knew he could not hold on any longer, and as he felt his right hand leave the stone, he closed his eyes, and tried to remember the faces of his mother and father.

Suddenly, claws dug into his shoulder. Then more grabbed high on his other arm and his lower legs. He opened his eyes and saw the rocks rushing towards him, then slipping away. Cold air rushed around him, making him shake and his teeth chatter.

The leathery wings of the bats brushed his back and legs, and he heard a deep crunching and smashing of rock behind him. The earth was shaking violently and looking beneath his arm, he saw the dark hulk of the fortress crumbling away, sliding and tumbling down the hill.

Panagati

Drishad sat on Ghandar high above the ruined city. From below, he could hear the sharp reports of axes as workers cleared the central avenue. Beneath him, at the base of the ramp, trowels scraped as masons began their repairs on Lord Ganesh's statue. He nudged Ghandar, and the gentle beast turned and joined the formation of courtiers and elephants before the archway of the salt cave.

Beth and Ryan were surrounded by the restored nobility of Rhamanapore. Elegant men and women in brightly colored clothing, sparkling with jewels, bowed as the cousins shuffled to the gaping cave. Vati rubbed Ryan's head with his trunk, making the hair stick up.

"Hey!" Ryan pushed the trunk away playfully, then patted it. Vati had several fresh scars from the horrible injuries he had endured at the gates of Karhada Keep. He and Ghandar had led a herd of bulls against Saudaheva. Enraged by the sorcerer, they had thrown down the gates, but were repulsed by the darkness and their injuries. Many of the elephants that ringed the children showed signs of the battle. Some that had greeted them when they emerged from this cave not long ago were no longer here to say good-bye.

The elephants parted to make way for Ghandar and the new Maharajah, dressed in long flowing silks and an elaborate robe. He wore the Maharajah's stone, discovered in the wreck of the palace, and his seat was placed on a large tiger skin draped on the back of the elephant. He wore a kingly gaze, but Drishad grinned at Beth and Ryan the same way he had when they met at the temple.

"I have here something to return to you," he said to Ryan, and Ghandar reached up with his trunk. The boy king produced the staff, which Ghandar lowered to Ryan. "A wood-cutter discovered this, after the hollow had drained. He had the wisdom to give your staff to the village priest, and now it has found the way back to you." Ryan looked at Beth.

"Tell him thanks for the gift. Now we might actually have a chance of getting back." Beth relayed Ryan's appreciation.

"It is not a gift. I am merely returning what was misplaced. *This* is a gift." He placed something else in Ghandar's trunk, and it was passed to Beth. Beth lifted up the gold chain with its enormous amber diamond.

"Uh… Thanks, Drishad. Don't you want this?"

"You will be doing me a favor by taking it. I want to be free of its curse. This city will be rebuilt anew, and my people will tame this jungle. We want a new home where we once belonged, a place dedicated to the old stories and our ancient ways. As long as I see that pendant, I will remember the evil of Saudaheva. No. Please take it with you. I will sleep better knowing it is no longer in my world. Magic has not been kind to my family."

"My clan will remain here as well," Ghandar rumbled. "Some will stay in the forest with my grandmother, but others are ready to make the legends come back to life. Madriva is too old to change, but I am not."

"She has honored her promise, and now I will try to honor mine," Drishad pronounced. "You have made all of this

possible, and I can only express again my eternal gratitude," Drishad bowed, and the courtiers followed suit.

"Thank you, Drish....Uh.... Maharajah." Beth was uncomfortable with the attention and she felt her cheeks glow.

"Let's go, Beth. We need to get back. They've probably given up on us by now."

"Yeah. O.K. Let's go."

The children waved farewell, shaking as many hands and patting as many trunks as they could reach. They felt sad as they walked to the back of the cave, but they were also anxious, hoping they would be home soon. The elephants trumpeted a deafening salute as they squeezed behind the boulder. They had fresh oil in their lamps, and they crept quickly down the tunnel as it bent deep into the earth.

Soon they came to a split in the cave. Ryan held out the staff as he had before.

"O.K. stick, this didn't work last time, but show us the way home." He dropped the staff and it clattered on the stone, pointing to the left. They continued, repeating the process at every crossing of caverns. The lamps began to feel light again, and Ryan started to worry. Beth turned around and stopped him.

"Did you hear that?" she whispered.

"No. You're always hearing things."

"And you're never hearing things until it's too late."

"That's not true, when we were…"

"Shhh… There it is again. Listen."

They sat very still, listening, but all they heard was an occasional dripping sound and the flickering hiss of their lamps. Ryan opened his mouth to say something, when he suddenly heard a very faint noise. He shut his mouth and nodded to Beth, who raised one eyebrow. They sat for a moment and waited. The sound grew nearer and louder. It was infrequent, coming once every few minutes, until they could finally make it out. It was a voice.

"Ya-heh!" The voice said.

"Hello!" Beth shouted, and her high-pitched voice echoed in the cavern.

"Ya-heh!" The voice called back immediately.

127

"What did you do that for?" Ryan whispered. "Who knows what that voice belongs to. We should wait and have a look."

"Ryan, after all the stuff we've been through, you're going to tell me to wait when I hear someone looking for us?"

"Maybe they're not looking for us. Maybe they're looking for something to eat. These caves creep me out. After all this, it could be anything."

"Ya-heh!"

There was no place to hide, and the voice was very close now. There was nothing to do but sit and wait. Then, a few feet ahead of them, they saw light coming from down the tunnel. They saw the outline of a figure, tall and bent. A dark shadow swung around the head. Then they both recognized the dark face at once.

"Laughing Cloud!" Beth shouted.

BACK TO THE PARK

"I felt your loss was my mistake. You don't have to apologize," Laughing Cloud said, as he pushed the heavy door closed. "I didn't tell you the whole truth about the caves, but we want to keep these places a secret. Some people might want them. They might take them away from us. You understand?" Beth and Ryan nodded. Laughing Cloud smiled.

He had found them not too far from the first split in the cave that had caused so much trouble. They had been missing for days, and everyone assumed they were gone forever. Laughing Cloud knew they had food, and suspected they might have come out somewhere. He had searched every day, and had almost given up hope. He had decided to retrace his steps and start from the beginning of the cave system. That's when he found them.

The stone house was bright and cheery. It was a new morning, and Laughing Cloud agreed to take them straight back to the park. Ryan handed the staff back to Laughing Cloud.

"This was very useful. I'm sorry I took your property without asking. I really had no idea."

"You didn't take the staff, Ryan. The staff took you. Thank you for returning it."

Beth dug in her pockets and gave him the acorn, the berries and the feather. Laughing Cloud nodded as she thanked him, but handed the berries back.

"This is not something I should use now. You keep them. I have many more."

"Can we go now, L.C.?" Ryan pleaded. The Oponowa laughed and they followed him out the door.

In the warm sunlight, they were able to travel much faster. Everything looked familiar, and both children were very happy they were almost home. The forest had lost its sinister edge, and Beth breathed deeply. Ryan marched close on Laughing Cloud's heels, and both children breathlessly told him the details of their story. After a few hours they had hiked to the edge of the wood and the park boundary.

"You are welcome here always," Laughing Cloud said. "You belong to the forest now. You have held the Council Staff and walked beneath the hill. You are people of the tree." He placed his hands first on Beth's shoulders and then Ryan's. "I will stay here. You go back to your home." Ryan shook his hand and Beth embraced the tall Oponowa. She barely came up to his chest.

"Oh. I almost forgot. I have something for you to keep in the root house." She pulled out Saudaheva's diamond on the chain and placed it in Laughing Cloud's palm. "I don't have anywhere to keep this safe." Laughing Cloud's face split wide with an enormous grin.

"I know this stone, although the chain is new. This was called 'The Eye of the Cat.' This will not be the first time the stone has been in the root house. I will keep it there for you, for when you return." He placed the flashing gem around his neck. "I will make my way home much easier with this." He belted out a great blast of laughter.

Beth and Ryan stepped over the fence where the great fallen limb pressed the wires down, trotting across the dirt road. They looked back to wave good-bye, but where Laughing Cloud had stood, there was an enormous black panther. He leapt up into the nearest tree, and climbed high into the limbs. Beth saw the eyes gleaming between the leaves. She blinked and he was gone.

They walked through the park and out the gates. The afternoon gave way to early evening, the heat of the day brushed aside by a cool breeze. Ryan looked at the rows of pleasant houses and asphalt streets, so different from the stone ruins of Panagati. The light greens of the well sprinkled grass looked pale as he remembered marching through the deep emerald jungles of Rhamanapore. The warm concrete of the sidewalk felt hard after the leafy floor of Council wood. Beth grinned, sauntering next to Ryan.

"We're really home."

"Yeah. But it feels different."

"I don't care. I think it's great. And you know what's best?"

"What?"

"None of those awful insects."

She gave his hand a squeeze and broke into a run. Ryan laughed and chased her. They raced home, cutting through the lawns.

The Author

Hap Arnold is a literary addict and an avid traveler. He writes in Louisville, Kentucky, after returning from several years in Europe and the Middle East. A fugitive from reality, he hides in a comfortable suburban box with his family, sheltered by a very old oak tree.

The Illustrator

Kieran Wathen is a scenic artist with a distinguished background in theatrical production. He currently haunts Old Louisville in a perpetually unfinished apartment. This is his first collaboration with the author.

COME WITH BETH AND RYAN
ON THEIR NEXT ADVENTURE...

THE SECRET OF
SPRING MILL

Ameenah handed Beth the skin of water she had brought. Her father had almost drained it, but there was a little bit at the bottom.

"I can take you to more," she said, as the two strangers shared the last few drops. "But you must promise not to hurt my family."

"We're not going to hurt anyone. We just want to get back home." Beth assured her. She smiled at Ameenah. Beth could tell she was a little older than Ryan. Something about her seemed like a grown up. Her eyes were dark and serious. She was tall, and her hands were rough from work. Her garments were simple and old. As she turned to lead them, Beth caught a glimpse of her profile. She was reminded strongly of the women drawn on the walls of the tomb.

Beth translated for Ryan, who followed them with the staff. He didn't look so well, his face was pasty and gray, and he kept his head bent as he shuffled along.

As they neared the mouth of the mine, it became warm. Beth and Ryan stripped off their heavy coats and carried them.

"I will not take you to the main tunnel. The guards will ask questions." Ameenah said, turning down a side passage. They emerged into sun and heat at the base of a rocky hill. The landscape was barren, without a hint of green. They trotted down a new path.

"Few come this way. This is an old cave, but a new mine. We just began digging here a few weeks ago."

"Are they looking for gold or something?" Ryan asked through Beth.

"My father thinks they are looking for something else. Something secret."

They followed Ameenah down into a crevice. She eased her way carefully into the rock, and filled her skin with water. She passed it back up to the other kids several times while they drank their fill. When they were refreshed, she led them down another path for some time.

After struggling up a hill they stood above a large town. It clung along the smooth bend of a wide, brown river. Tall palms and green fields surrounded a hive of small huts, and several great buildings of stone were clumped together to the North, separate from the rest of the city.

"Well," Ryan grumbled. "Not much familiar here."

"It's very beautiful," Beth muttered to Ryan. The sun was setting and the stone was orange and pink. Long dark fingers of shadow made the city look exotic and mysterious.

"Things in this Nome are not what they once were. I imagine my father would like to speak with you about it. He may be able to help you." Ameenah flashed a brilliant smile. "I am certain he will have many questions for you. If you will come to my home, you may eat and rest there." At the mention of rest, the muscles in Beth's legs turned to rubber. She had no idea how long they had been gone, but she was ready to collapse.

Ameenah led them through the town, careful to use quiet streets where they would not be noticed. It was impossible to avoid the main avenue for a short way, and many heads turned to stare at Beth and Ryan's strange garb. Only a block from her street, she heard the beat of drums, and saw the crowd in front part, like reeds before the wind. It was too late to make it out of the way. As Ameenah hurried, pulling the strangers behind, the grand procession came into view. She had no choice but to fall to her knees and bow her head, dragging the others with her.

Beth and Ryan could not bow their heads, they were too busy watching. Their jaws hung open in disbelief as the procession drew nearer. First were the jackal headed bodyguards, snapping leather whips to clear the way. They didn't wear masks, what they carried on their necks were the actual snapping, snarling, drooling heads of wild dogs. Behind them, carried in a sedan chair, another horror crouched. The long green snout and twisted teeth of a great reptile was set on the shoulders of a hulking, muscular man. The crocodile man squeezed a sponge full of water over his hideous face, and the green skin glistened. Ryan saw the lizard's eyes squeeze shut against the sun, as it appeared to doze.

Behind this monster was a more elaborate chair, and Beth caught her breath when she glimpsed the next attraction. Half man, half bird, its beak was partly open as it squawked harshly to the lizard in front. The black feathers, ruffled and unkempt, surrounded quick, beady eyes. The bird man's gaze was dark as midnight.

"It's a raven," Beth muttered.

"It's a crow, Beth. A crow." Ryan whispered back. As he stared at the twisted bird, fire licked across his forearm. The rabid face of a jackal snarled at him, foam streaking its jowls, as it raised the whip for another blow. Ryan shouted in pain, and Ameenah yanked him down to the street, saving him from further damage. The three children crouched in a huddle and heard the procession shuffle by. Ryan stole a last glimpse at the ruffled black feathers on the back of the half-bird's head.

"Crow," Ryan snarled to himself. "What is he up to?"